RUTHLESS SURRENDER

THE SURRENDER SERIES, BOOK ONE

ZOE BLAKE

Poison Ink Publications

Copyright © 2018, 2021 by Zoe Blake & Poison Ink Publications

All rights reserved.

No part of this book may be reproduced in any form or by any electronic or mechanical means, including information storage and retrieval systems, without written permission from the author, except for the use of brief quotations in a book review.

Cover Design by Dark City Designs

CONTENTS

Chapter 1	1
Chapter 2	9
Chapter 3	14
Chapter 4	27
Chapter 5	34
Chapter 6	52
Chapter 7	61
Chapter 8	69
Chapter 9	79
Chapter 10	94
Chapter 11	111
Chapter 12	116
Chapter 13	122
Epilogue	147
About Zoe Blake	153
Also by Zoe Blake	155

CHAPTER 1

How deep does a grave have to be?

Wasn't there something about animals?

Chloe gripped the small heart charm that hung about her neck, taking solace as the metal warmed beneath her hand. The blue-white beam of her flashlight bounced off dark tree trunks and the thick bed of wet leaves and twigs that covered the ground.

Would the rain make digging easier or harder, she wondered?

The sound of crunching gravel alerted her to a car traveling up the long driveway even before she saw the headlights. Turning off her flashlight, she ran back toward the cabin, tripping over a half-buried log in her haste. Throwing open the rough wooden gate that separated the forest from the clearing, she raced across the yard, ignoring the ice-cold rain that drenched her and seeped into her sneakers as her feet sank into the rain-soaked grass. Cringing at the loud squeak the back screen door made as she carefully opened it, Chloe locked it behind

1

her and crouched low as she crossed the study into the kitchen. Keeping her head down, she reached up and turned off the small lamp she always kept lit on her kitchen table. Without the soft warm glow, the cabin felt cold and still.

Chloe held her breath, straining to hear the sound of any movement outside. A car door. The sound of an engine turning off. If there was a God, the sound of gravel as the car turned around and left.

Silence.

The anxiety of not knowing was too much. Chloe crawled across the linoleum, around the kitchen island. She paused and listened.

Still nothing.

Trying to calm her pounding heart, she crept closer to the front door. Her knees ached from crawling on the hard floor. Her soaked jeans chafed and clung to her hips with every movement. She could feel mud squishing between her toes inside her sneakers. All she wanted was to take a hot shower and forget that this night had ever happened. But that wasn't possible. She could never wash away the horror of this night.

Grimacing as small pebbles tracked inside from the driveway cut into the palms of her hands, Chloe slowly crept into the mud room. The front door was straight ahead. It had a windowpane but no curtain or shade, so she kept low and to the shadows. Just beyond was the small porch and the gravel drive. Leaning against the wall to the right of the door, Chloe tilted her head and listened.

More silence.

Her heartbeat finally slowed.

It must have been a neighbor driving by.

"Chloe. Open the door."

Throwing her hand over her mouth to stifle a scream, Chloe scurried farther back along the wall, staring at the closed door with wild eyes.

There was another long, excruciating pause.

Then.

"I know you are in there. I need you to open the door."

The dark command of his voice almost had her obeying. How did this man know her name? Who was he? The police? She would have welcomed the police. An hour ago. But not now. Now it was too late. Maybe he was a friend of *his*. Just another reason why she couldn't open the door. The cabin was dark. The doors locked. Her car was parked in the garage with the door closed. There was no real way for him to know she was inside. Maybe if she stayed quiet, he would give up and leave?

"Baby, I'm losing my patience. Trust me. You don't want that."

The deep tone of the stranger's voice was getting harsher. Did she dare continue to defy him?

She moved her hand over the low shelf that ran along the wall at her back, encountering bug candles, rubber boots, and fishing tackle. Nothing that could be used as a weapon. There were her late uncle's hunting rifles in the gun cabinet in the living room, but she would have to crawl back through the kitchen to get to them. The cabin was dark, but there was no way he would not see the outline of her movements through the front door window now that he was standing just on the other side. The door wasn't even secured with a deadbolt, just a simple key lock. She lived in a cabin in the woods in the middle of nowhere in upstate Michigan where all the neighbors knew one another. There wasn't a need for extraneous locks and deadbolts.

"I'm giving you one last chance to open this door, babygirl," the stranger growled.

Chloe knew the old door with its old lock would not hold. She needed to make a decision.

The door handle rattled violently.

She was out of time.

Jumping up, Chloe bolted back through the kitchen.

The sickening sound of splintering wood and shattering glass reverberated throughout the cabin.

Chloe's wet soles skidded along the floor as she sharply turned right down the narrow hallway to the living room. The gun cabinet was just over the threshold. Her trembling hand closed over the cabinet door's brass handle. The guns weren't loaded, but hopefully the stranger wouldn't get close enough to notice. Wrenching the handle upwards, Chloe threw open the cabinet door and blindly reached in, feeling for the cold barrel of the rifle she knew was there.

A hand closed over her shoulder, spinning her about and slamming her against the wall. She had no chance to even scream. That same hand wrapped around her throat, the long fingers easily encircling the slender column till her jaw was pushed upwards, her head crushed painfully against the wall.

The sharp angles of the stranger's face came into focus. His angry, lowered brow. Dark, unreadable eyes.

His full lips lifted in a snarl. "I warned you, baby."

Chloe tried to rise up on her toes to ease the pressure on her throat. Desperately, she clawed at the man's T-shirt. A garbled scream escaped her lips.

"Shhh… all that will do is piss me off more than I already am, and we don't want that, do we?" He leaned in close to whisper the ominous threat, his lips skimming along her jaw. The scrape of his stubble rubbed against the soft skin of her cheek.

She tried to shake her head no, but his grip on her throat would not allow it.

He spread his legs wide before tilting his hips forward, pressing into her body. He was a large beast of a man. Both his size and voice were frightening. Intimidating.

He ran the back of his knuckles down her cheek. "Now, you are going to be a good girl and obey me."

Chloe tried to convey her willingness with her eyes.

He seemed to understand because he released his grip on her throat but shifted his hips as if to remind her he still held a portion of her body prisoner. As if she needed reminding.

With a warning look in her direction, he flicked on the switch by her shoulder.

Chloe blinked as the room flooded with light. The moment her eyes had adjusted, she got her first real look at the stranger who had forced his way into her cabin. If he had not been holding her against the wall, her knees would have given out in sheer fright. Jesus Christ! The man looked like the type of prison thug you only saw in the movies…or mug shots on the news. Impossibly tall, his chest and arms were thick with muscle. He had a neck tattoo. *A goddamn neck tattoo.* Piercing blue eyes watched her with amusement.

"You like what you see, babygirl?"

Oh God, thought Chloe. She had survived one horror this night only to end up being raped and murdered by this man.

Maybe it was what she deserved.

He ran a finger over her collarbone and then traced the V-neck edge of her pink T-shirt.

Chloe bit her lip to keep from crying out. Her fists were clenched so hard, her palms hurt from where her fingernails bit into them.

Still he taunted her. His finger slowly ran up and down the edge of her neckline, till it dipped into the low vee. Hooking his finger into the flimsy, damp fabric, he pulled it toward him.

Chloe cried out in alarm and started to raise her arms in defense.

"Don't," he ordered.

She had no choice but to lower them helplessly to her sides.

Her T-shirt gaped open, exposing her to his intense gaze.

Chloe closed her eyes in mortification. The generous top curves of her breasts, encased in delicate white lace, were clearly on display. A small pink design was embroidered right in the center of her bra, nestling in her cleavage.

The stranger raised one dark eyebrow. "Hello Kitty?"

Chloe slowly nodded her head.

"Later I'm going to want a closer look at this cute bra, but for now, we have some business to attend to."

A warm tear escaped the corner of her eye. *Later?* Her stomach twisted.

Her cabin was isolated and hard to reach during the day, let alone during a torrential storm in the middle of the night. Even if she were willing to call the police, they would never reach her in time. It would take Glennie's small force at least an hour to respond to her call for help. She shuddered to think what this dangerous man could do to her in the span of an hour.

"Please," she choked out. "The stones are in my office. In the safe."

"Stones?"

"The diamonds. Just take them."

The man chuckled, the sinister sound devoid of any mirth.

"I don't give a fuck about any diamonds."

"Then what do you want?"

The moment the question left her lips, she knew it was a mistake.

The man leaned in with his hips. The hard ridge of his arousal pressed against her stomach.

Chloe whimpered as she shifted her body to the side, desperately trying to break his hold.

What kind of man turned down diamonds? A crazy fuck, that's who.

Chloe didn't trust anyone who claimed to not be interested in money. Money was cold, unfeeling. Straightforward. Every horrible moment in her fucked up, twisted life could be traced back to someone else's need for money. At least it made things uncomplicated. There was no wondering about a reason, no need for deep self-reflection or even that elusive idea of closure or meaning. She knew why. It was money. Always money.

There was only one other thing besides money that could influence a person's actions. Sex.

She could feel the ominous power of his *intention* as he used his body to cage hers.

She would not give in without a fight. Clenching her small hand into a fist, she lashed out. The fifteen carat, vintage amethyst ring she always wore caught him on the cheekbone. A droplet of blood trickled from the scratch caused by one of the diamond accents.

He raised two fingertips to swipe at the blood. Keeping his eyes trained on hers, his tongue flicked out to taste the crimson drop.

Watching him, she could almost taste the metallic tang on her own tongue.

"I was hoping you would fight me. It will make this all so much easier."

Her scream was lost in the deep, dark woods.

CHAPTER 2

Logan placed his hand over her mouth. "You need to knock that shit off, or I'll shut your mouth up another way."

He was almost disappointed when she complied. He would have liked to have had an easy excuse to press his cock past those pink, lip-glossed lips of hers. From the stubborn glint in her eyes, Logan was sure she would give him another reason soon.

After all, she had information he needed, and he was prepared to get it by any means necessary.

"Good girl," he said as he removed his hand. "Now, are you going to continue to be nice and obedient for me, and tell me everything I want to know?"

She looked downward, hiding her soft gray eyes from him, before nodding.

"That's strike one," he warned.

Startled eyes rose again as her sweet mouth opened on a gasp.

"Let's try this again. Perhaps I wasn't being direct enough. Where the fuck is Chad?"

Her head jerked when he said the name. From his position, pressed along her body, he could feel her short, rapid breaths as her chest rose and fell.

"I… I… don't know anyone named Chad." Her voice was low and hoarse.

"That's strike two."

She paused as her eyes flicked back downward. Licking her lips, she repeated her previous lie. "Please. I'm telling you the truth. I don't know anyone named Chad."

"And that's three."

Logan leaned back and grabbed her thin T-shirt in both hands. Wrenching the garment upwards, he forced her arms up high. Keeping the damp, pink fabric around her wrists, he ruthlessly twisted it tight, effectively securing them.

"No! No! Stop!" she screamed as she twisted her hips and helplessly pulled against his impromptu binding of her wrists.

Fisting the fabric between her bound wrists, Logan shifted his weight. Raising his knee, he pressed it high between her legs. The moment his knee made contact with her jean-clad cunt, she stilled, like a rabbit caught in a predator's snare.

With his free hand, Logan reached down inside his black biker boot to withdraw the bowie knife he always kept handy.

"Oh God! Please don't kill me," she pleaded.

"Shh…" he soothed.

He pressed the blade against her soft skin, slipping it

under her left bra strap. Carefully twisting the blade, the knife easily sliced through the thin elastic.

His captive whimpered but stayed still.

Logan sucked air sharply through his clenched teeth. Jesus, he liked the sound of her frightened mews as her body nervously shifted against his own. He could just imagine the vibrations of that same whimper against his cock as he forced it deep down her throat. Or how she would sound pleading with him to stop as he strapped that plump, curved ass of hers with his belt. She was a pretty little package. Large gray eyes were framed with thick black lashes. High cheekbones were tinted a bright pink. Her dark brown hair was the color of leather, just long enough for a man to grab and wrap around his fist.

Logan flicked his wrist and quickly cut her other bra strap.

The thin lace material immediately sagged under the soft weight of her breasts, clinging only to the tips, denying him a look at her nipples. Would they be pink like her lips or darker, he wondered?

He placed the end of the knife between her breasts, pressing the metal tip to her skin, although careful not to draw blood. Slowly, he sliced through the cartoon kitten in the center. The fabric gave with a snap. The lace cups fell away, exposing her generous curves to his gaze.

She turned her head toward the wall, squeezing her eyes shut as tiny white teeth bit down on her plump lower lip.

Momentarily releasing his hold on the T-shirt that secured her wrists, Logan adjusted his stance and pierced the wet fabric with his knife, driving the blade deeply into the wall. Once again, she was immobile. Bound. Vulnerable.

Her skin felt cool and damp to his touch as he placed both hands on her breasts, cupping each underside curve.

Her head swung violently back. Her beautiful eyes narrowed in a defiant glare. He watched as she tested the binds on her wrists. The wet, twisted T-shirt held tight. He could feel the muscles of her right thigh tense. Sensing her next move, he swiftly placed his knee back between her legs.

"Can't have you kneeing the jewels, babygirl. I would be no good to you later," he quipped. "Let's try this again." Logan lightly pinched her left nipple between his forefinger and thumb. "Where is Chad?"

Her voice faltered as she murmured, "I don't know where he is."

"Progress. You at least admit you know him. The problem, baby," Logan leaned in close as he whispered against her open lips, "is I can tell you're still lying to me." He gave her pert nipple a quick twist.

Chloe cried out, though he figured it was more from surprise than pain as he knew he wasn't twisting that hard.

"People have all sorts of tells. A lowered gaze, a long pause before responding." Logan caressed the pulse point at the base of her throat with the side of his thumb. "Rapid breath."

The delicate skin of her throat fluttered under the slight pressure of his thumb. Her breath quick and short.

"I have already given you more than three strikes.

Trust me. You don't want to know what happens if you lie to me one more time."

Logan ran the back of his knuckles down the slope of her breast. They were just to his taste. More than a handful but not too big. He liked when they were big enough to bounce when he had a woman on top riding his cock, but still high and perky. He rolled her nipple between his fingers. A subtle threat of more pain.

"That piece of shit you call an ex-boyfriend was headed here, Chloe. Now, if you are hiding him…."

"He can rot in hell. I'm not hiding that bastard." Chloe ground out her response between clenched teeth.

"But you are still lying to me. Now, you either tell me where he is…or things are going to get very pleasurable for me, but rough for you."

Another threat. This one not the least bit subtle.

The little minx stubbornly turned her head away. Her pink lips pressed into a straight line.

Logan's brow lowered as he ran the tip of his tongue over the sharp edges of his teeth, the slight scrape of pain keeping him grounded. She may not be innocent in this mess, but he still needed to be careful. She had information he needed. Information he would do anything to learn. Anything.

His hand lowered to his jeans.

Pulling his thick leather belt through the clasp of the heavy belt buckle, Logan's eyes pierced his unwilling captive's. "It's time you learn what happens to bad girls who lie."

CHAPTER 3

Earlier that evening

CHLOE RUBBED HER NECK. She had been bent over her JoolTool, polishing for over an hour. The soft whirring noise filled her small second story studio. She looked at the metal clay molds scattered about her workbench. Her latest design was a large silver sugar skull pendant. Its eyes and design features were filled with small precious stones. The boutique she worked with in New York had already placed an order for two hundred. It would take her two solid weeks to fill the requisition. It was quiet, solitary work, and she preferred it that way.

Considering the loud chaos of her life a couple of years ago, spending time alone in the woods working on her jewelry designs was a heaven she didn't deserve.

Her mind flashed back to those years. What she remembered most was the blood. A bright crimson. The sickening metallic smell of it. The more it flowed, the slower and softer the begging became. The words becoming slurred and thick like the dark, sickly flow of red.

Giving herself a shake, Chloe's eyes sought the view outside her glass French doors. The pristine lake with its ducks and geese gently floating on the rippling surface always had a calming effect. Time had slipped away from her. The warm glow of afternoon had waned into a cold, dark drizzling rain. Instead of a view of the lake, her own reflection looked back at her in the dark glass. With her hair pulled back into a tight ponytail, Chloe's high cheekbones gave her face a sunken, tired appearance. A dark sullen look to match her dark sullen mood.

Deep down she knew she was lying to herself. Her reflection told a truth she was too much of a coward to admit to herself. She was restless and bored. While she didn't miss many things about her old life, she did miss the rush, the energy, the madness of it. She knew it wouldn't be long before she did something rash, something ill-advised, just to calm her agitated soul. She was chafing at her self-imposed bonds of boring respectability. Hating the weight of responsibility, only the guilt she felt kept her in line and, with each day, its hold on her slipped.

With a resigned sigh, she gathered up the small trays of precious stones and walked over to the massive black safe that lurked in the corner. Punching in the six-digit code, she waited till she heard the thunk of the latch releasing before grasping the cold metal handle. Wrenching it clockwise, she opened the heavy door.

Averting her eyes from the old, purple Crown Royal bag bunched to the side, Chloe placed the trays inside the safe and locked it.

She took the steps two at a time down to the first floor. Her studio was above the garage, which was a separate cabin from her home. She looked about the pristine space. Every wall was covered in white cabinets and drawers, each one carefully labeled. She and her uncle had shared the same love of organization. Gloves, maps, flares, ammunition. He had used this property as a hunting retreat. There was the main house, the garage with the loft space above, a shed for preparing any game killed and another cabin which was an informal bunkhouse. It had been a godsend when he'd offered it to her to stay after… well, after.

Reaching up for the metal chain to the single light bulb, she pulled it, pitching the large space into darkness. Shaking off a chill of apprehension, she headed for the welcoming glow of the main cabin. It was silly, but she always kept the lamp on the kitchen table lit. It gave the illusion someone was waiting for her when she got home. Preferring some solitude, and coming home to the cold, damp feeling of a dark home, were two different things. Knowing her thin T-shirt would be no match for the light drizzle, Chloe bolted for the cover of the front porch. Opening the door she always kept unlocked, she stepped into the cramped mud room. As she closed the door and kicked off her sneakers, the sound of clinking glass came from inside.

Without thinking, she raced through the open door into the tiny kitchen. There was a male form standing in front of her open fridge, hanging onto the door as he rummaged through the various containers and bottles.

"Jesus fucking Christ, Chloe. You never change. Nothing but half-empty Chinese food containers. I ate better behind bars."

The man opened one cardboard container and, after taking a sniff, turned and began opening drawers till he found a fork. Piercing a large bite of lo mein, he shoved the whole thing in his mouth. Sickening slurping noises filled the silent room.

Chloe stood there frozen in horror.

He had found her.

It had been a risk going to family for help, but she had never talked about her uncle to him. Tucking herself away in the isolated woods of upstate Michigan was as far away from the crowds and noise of Louisiana as she could get. Besides, he was supposed to still be in prison. She took in the dark blue jeans and the white sweatshirt stamped with Daniel Wade Correctional Center. Apparently, he had been until recently.

"You escaped?" Her voice sounded hollow and breathless.

He gave her a wink. "Always the smart one. Let's just say I secured my own early release."

Chloe placed a hand on the kitchen island to keep the room from spinning. "How?"

"A lonely woman who comes to the prison to bring color and art to us poor, corrupt souls and an unguarded ventilation shaft." His response was dismissive.

Chloe felt a brief stab of pity for the unknown woman.

Her life was probably now ruined because she'd fallen for Chad's charms. Just another notch in his belt.

"I didn't hear you drive up." It was an inane statement, but she needed a moment to process his presence in her sanctuary.

"Piece of shit I stole ran out of gas just outside of town. Walked the rest of the way," he said with his mouth full of Chinese food.

"But how did you find me?"

Chad had turned back to rummaging in the fridge, opening containers. "What? You think you're clever or something?" He shook his head with a look of disgust on his face. "You think you're so smart. Wills are public record, you dumb bitch. A quick Internet search was all it took to find your dead uncle's shack in the woods."

Chloe closed her eyes, blocking out the sight of him but not his words or the memories.

"Chad, you can't be here. The cops will be looking for you."

"I spent three years behind bars because of you, bitch. I'm not going anywhere till I get what I came for."

She felt the familiar twist of tension in her stomach. She had covered her tracks so well. There was no way he knew she'd been the one who'd taken the diamonds, that she'd been the one who'd ratted him out to Internal Affairs. Chloe took a step back, taking comfort from the feel of the solid wall behind her back.

His long, greasy blond hair was tucked behind his ears. Years spent inside had cost him his dark tan, but his body was still lean with muscle. Those brown eyes she'd once thought were so beautifully mesmerizing looked watery and unfocused. He was high.

A sober Chad was as mean as a snake, but a high Chad? *Much worse.*

Keeping her shoulders pressed to the wall, she slid her right foot to the side. One tiny step.

"I… I don't have anything of yours, Chad. I gave everything to your brother before I left."

One more tiny step to the right.

"Left? Left? You mean skipped town. Leaving me with no alibi. Do you have any idea how pissed Jose was when he found out I had left the shit with you?"

Jose had been Chad's gang connection when he'd been a dirty cop down in Louisiana. Chad would skim product off the top of any drug bust then, for a cut, give it to Jose to sell back on the streets. Only problem was that Chad got greedy. Started taking more and more and his bosses had become suspicious. Internal Affairs had started asking questions. Chad, once a great boyfriend, became more and more violent and erratic as he started to sample the product himself. Things got bloody.

And Chloe had started to plan her escape.

She'd taken only what could fit in the back of her car and had gotten the hell out of there. Chad had been relying on her to lie to the police and give him an alibi for that night. Instead, she'd told Internal Affairs everything she knew and left with the diamonds. The damn diamonds. They had been a side job of Chad's. He'd thought no one knew about them, and he was almost right. The police hadn't made him for that job, but she'd known about them, and where he had hidden them.

They were supposed to be her ticket out. She had been going to use the money to go to Europe. Start a new life. Turned out she needn't have bothered. The damn stones were S11s, with excessive clouds and pinpoints, and were practically worthless. Leave it to Chad to go to all the trouble of stealing diamonds that even a cheap jewelry store would sell for drill bit parts. Still, she kept them as a reminder. A reminder of the time she'd sunk to her lowest level.

Two years later and she still hadn't shaken off the guilt. The feeling she should have been punished for what she'd done, and hadn't done, still remained. She'd known Chad was dirty, and she'd looked the other way. There was something about the danger, the kick in the teeth to society's rules, that had thrilled her. Besides, no one was really getting hurt, right?

Wrong.

Chad dropped the Chinese food container on the counter, not giving a shit when sauce splattered on the tile surface. Turning his back on her, he examined the still-open fridge. "No beer. Of course."

Chloe took the chance and slid to her right again. Reaching blindly, her hand closed on the smooth plastic of her wall phone. Cell phones were unreliable and practically useless this deep in the woods. Lifting the phone off the cradle, she prepared to lock herself in the bathroom just around the corner and call the police. It would mean awkward questions and gossip. Word would spread quickly throughout the small town. She would have to leave her cozy haven.

"What the fuck do you think you're doing?"

His angry shout was her only warning.

There was a crushing pain in the lower part of her ribs. Her lungs seized. Striking the hard floor with her knees, she collapsed to her side. Her mouth opened grotesquely wide as she struggled to suck in air.

She watched helplessly as Chad placed his booted foot on her hair, pinning her to the floor, a trapped butterfly.

"You're going to tell me where you hid my shit, bitch, or I'll fucking kick you to death."

The squeezing pain in her lungs would not allow her to scream as she watched his other foot shift backwards. Her eyes rolled back. She passed out before the first kick.

* * *

DISORIENTED, Chloe opened her eyes. Splaying her fingers, she felt the gritty surface of her kitchen's linoleum floor. Pushing herself up on her elbow, she gingerly tried to rise to her feet. Her ribs and stomach were sore but not overly so. He must have only just punched her. The kick a threat. A threat he had carried through on in the past. Unwillingly, her mind returned to that other night. Chad had beaten a child to force that child's father to give up information on where some large cache of cocaine was hidden. Beaten the poor kid. Right in front of Chloe. Then he'd kicked her when she'd tried to intervene, and that had only been the beginning.

Blood. Bright crimson blood.

He should have been put in jail for the rest of his life for what he'd done that night. Instead, he'd flipped on some gang leaders and corrupt officials, pulled some strings and had gotten a slap on the wrist. Five years in a minimum security prison, Daniel Wade Correction Center in Claiborne Parish. A prison filled with dirty cops and dirtier politicians. He'd probably made more connections than he'd lost by going in, and was now more dangerous than ever.

Chad was a blight. A threat to decent people. As long as he lived, she would never be free of her past.

There were some thudding noises coming from the small study just off the kitchen. Then the sound of breaking glass.

Chloe forced herself to her feet. Gripping the doorjamb for support, its harsh edge digging into her palm, she peered into the darkened room.

Chad was tossing the place. Books, knick-knacks and a broken picture frame lay scattered on the floor.

"Where the fuck are they?" he shouted.

Once again, her stomach knotted. She had taken the diamonds before he'd had a chance to try and fence them. He probably thought they were actually worth something. If she gave him the diamonds, there was no guarantee he would leave. It might make him even angrier if he had proof she had absolutely betrayed him and angrier still when he realized the diamonds were practically worthless. He might start drawing conclusions about her role with Internal Affairs. No matter what, she couldn't admit she had the diamonds. His reaction was too uncertain. The risk too great. If she let him continue to search the house, it would buy her some time to try to get the police. Perhaps he wouldn't even think to search the garage.

"I swear to God, bitch. The second I find those fucking

stupid toys of yours I'm going to break your goddamn neck for making me look for them." Chad continued to curse and mumble under his breath as he upended a small trunk of blankets she kept next to her reading chair.

Toys?

He wasn't making sense. It had probably taken him close to a week to reach her from Louisiana. By the looks of him, he was more concerned with getting a quick score than eating or showering. His movements were sharp and erratic. His ramblings disjointed and confused. She caught the word *kill* and *bitch* more than once.

Chloe knew with absolute certainty he was going to finish what he'd started two years ago on that dark night.

"Chad, how about I fix you something to eat?" Her voice sounded high-pitched and hollow from her forced cheerfulness.

"You? Cook? I'd rather eat prison food." His harsh words were given in a scathing snarl.

"Fine. How about a drink then. Whiskey, right?"

"Yeah. Yeah," he responded, distractedly. His eyes were wild from whatever he was on. "Then you're going to show me where you stashed my shit."

Chloe stepped back into the kitchen. Spinning around, she searched for a weapon. She looked at the set of knives in the knife block, an obvious choice, but no. He would overpower her before she got two steps near him. There were her uncle's hunting rifles in the living room gun cabinet, but none of them were loaded. Think. Think! There had to be something she could use.

She opened the freezer and made a racket pulling out

the ice trays. She then loudly opened and closed cabinet doors so he wouldn't get suspicious.

Think!

She forced her scared and scattered mind to focus. There was one thing. It might not work, but it was her only option.

Calling out to Chad, she said, "There are a few boxes I never unpacked in the back of my closet in the bedroom."

Chad stormed into the kitchen. He grabbed her upper arm in a painfully tight grip. "It's about time you started being useful, you dumb bitch. Where's my drink?"

"I'm getting it now."

He let go of her arm and stalked into the darkened bedroom.

Chloe waited till he was out of sight then dashed into the bathroom. With shaking hands, she carefully opened the medicine cabinet door, not wanting Chad to hear a sound. Reaching for an old pill bottle, she scurried back into the kitchen. Making sure to clink the glasses as she pulled one down, she opened the pill bottle. Her uncle's prescription for secobarbital. His "little red devils" as he called them. Chloe remembered them as the drug from that book, *Valley of the Dolls*. Hearing the sounds of boxes being torn open in the next room, she dumped the pills onto her wooden carving board. Ten pills, each 100 mg. Would it be enough? Maybe she would get lucky, and the whiskey and cocaine already coursing through his veins would take up any slack. Using a large spoon, she crushed the pills then mixed the pinkish powder into at least three fingers of whiskey. It would taste bitter and looked a bit cloudy. Fortunately, she knew Chad was never one to sip and take his time with something pleasurable. He grabbed. He consumed. He gulped. It was true in the bedroom and out, she remembered with a wry twist of her lips.

Tucking a small paring knife into her back pocket in case things went awry, her bare feet felt cold as she hesitantly crossed the kitchen into the master bedroom. She had to call out his name twice before he emerged from the walk-in closet. He looked ridiculous. His hair was sticking up all over. A pair of pantyhose was stuck to his sleeve, and in his hand he held a single leopard print pump. Still, Chloe knew better than to laugh or comment.

The ice rattled in the glass as her shaking hand held it out to him.

True to form, Chad seized it, tossing the contents back without sparing it a glance.

Wiping his mouth with the back of his hand, he threw the glass at Chloe. She only just avoided being hit in the head. "Fuck, that tastes like shit. What kind of cheap, bullshit whiskey do you keep in this joint? Get me vodka this time."

Chloe turned as if in a daze. She walked back into the kitchen and just stood there. Waiting. She could hear the pounding of her heart in her ears. Her fingers felt cold and numb. Still she waited. The sounds of Chad tossing her closet continued. Still she waited. She swayed a bit on her feet. The adrenaline pumping through her body was making her nauseated and dizzy.

She gave out a cry of fright when Chad appeared in the doorway.

His step was unsteady as he pointed a finger at her. "You! I know what you are up to!" he accused.

Chloe reached back for the plastic grip of the small knife she had in her jeans pocket.

"You can't footh me, you dump pitch. Youth thunk yous zo cleever."

Chad's words were slurred and indistinct. The drug was working.

Chloe just stared, silent. Had he guessed she'd spiked his drink? Would he kill her now?

"Thud toys ars in the study. Youth thaut to footh me."

He stumbled across the kitchen back into the study. She could hear his heavy footsteps as they crunched on the broken glass from the picture frame.

She waited, barely daring to breathe.

Had it been an hour? Five minutes? Thirty?

She had no concept of how long she stood silent in the kitchen. Holding her breath.

Waiting.

In the other room, she heard Chad cry out in alarm. There was a loud crash.

The sound of a body hitting the floor.

Dead weight.

Then…silence.

Chloe lifted the bottle of whiskey and took a long drink. The burn from the liquid finally snapped her out of her stupor.

Her ordeal was not over.

She now had a body to bury.

CHAPTER 4

There was something about the smooth weight of a thick leather strap in his hand that always made his dick hard. He was looking forward to disciplining this particular stubborn little piece.

He knew more about Chloe Taylor than her own mother did. Born in a small town outside of Chicago, it hadn't been long before Chloe's mother had dumped her in the lap of her elderly grandmother. The grandmother raised Chloe as best she could, but Chloe spent long stints in foster care as the elderly woman was in and out of hospitals till her death when Chloe was seventeen. By then it was too late; the girl had grown up wild. No discipline. Relishing in defying authority, always skirting the law, careless about school and any kind of future. There was an uncle barely in the picture. Career military. Rarely saw the niece but did come through when she needed a place to stay. Wound up leaving her the cabin in his will when he'd died late last year.

And then there was Chad. The loser ex-boyfriend.

Chloe had followed him to Louisiana. As far as Logan could tell, the only reason Chad had become a cop was for the power trip and the easy access to drugs. The guy was a real asshole. Logan was unclear about how complicit Chloe had been in Chad's exploits, but he did know she'd skipped town with more than just those cheap diamonds she'd offered him earlier.

Knowing Chad would be after the same thing he was, Logan had learned all about Chloe. Studied her. Even now there was a well-worn photograph of her in his back pocket. She was in ponytails, giving the camera a stubborn glare over her shoulder, as if she resented the intrusion of whoever was behind the lens into her private space.

It was her eyes that had first caught his attention.

No matter how many old Facebook posts and photos he flipped through to learn about his quarry, no matter what she was doing or what expression she was wearing…her eyes remained the same.

They always had this far-away pained look in their deep, gray depths. As if she were just going through the motions of happiness.

Lost.

A little girl lost.

But now she had been found by him.

* * *

"Look. Whatever you had going on with Chad, I wasn't involved. I swear to you! I don't know anything about his… his… business dealings."

"You know more than you're telling. I think you just need the proper motivation."

He watched the slender column of her throat contract as she nervously swallowed. Her long fingers kept flexing and moving as her wrists twisted against his binding.

Laying his belt to the side, Logan pressed his chest against her bare breasts as he reached over her to grip the bone handle of his knife. With a sharp pull, the knife slid from its deep mooring inside the wall. Before she could give a sigh of relief, Logan grasped her shoulder and flipped her around, crushing her breasts against the wall.

"What are you doing?" she screamed.

Once more, he drove the knife into her twisted T-shirt, securing her wrists high above her head.

Leaning in close, his teeth nipped at the delicate curve of her ear. She instantly stilled. "Teaching you a lesson."

Grasping her hip with one large hand to steady her, he forced his other hand between her waist and the wall. With a flick of his thumb and forefinger, he undid the small brass button of her jeans.

"No! No! No!"

She started to twist her hips, her bottom pushing out, brushing his already hard cock.

"Yes!" he ground out as he pulled down her zipper.

Her still wet and muddy jeans clung to her hips. Holding onto the denim waistband, he yanked them over her hip bones, exposing the curves of her pink, panty-clad bottom. He placed his big, black boot on the inside crotch of her jeans and forced the fabric down over her legs.

"Don't do this! Please! Don't!" Her voice warbled as she started to cry.

Logan left the damp denim clinging to her ankles, knowing it would prevent her from kicking out at his shins.

Ignoring her pleas, Logan ran one hand down her slim thigh. Her skin felt cold and damp. He would soon warm her up.

He placed his other hand on her lower back. Enjoying how it curved in slightly only to swell out into the upper curve of her ass. He forced two fingers into the thin fabric of her panties. Pulling the fabric outward, he skimmed his fingers along the ruffled elastic as he glimpsed the dark seam of her ass.

The soft damp curls of her hair brushed against his cheek as he leaned over her shoulder, feathering his lips along her jawline. "Tell me. Is there a Hello Kitty on the front of these pretty panties of yours?"

She remained stubbornly silent.

Logan raised his free hand and brought it swiftly down on her left bottom cheek. The crack of his open palm on her delicate skin echoed around the room.

She cried out, and he could feel her whole body jerk from the impact. Looking down, he could see the outline of his fingers slowly blossom on the undercurve of her ass and upper thigh, a dark pink against her white skin.

"I'll just have to see for myself."

Grabbing the flimsy fabric, he twisted his fist till the elastic snapped. There was the sound of fabric rending, then her panties fell limp against his palm. A Hello Kitty decal was distorted in their wrinkled folds.

"Why are you doing this to me?"

Her tears had brought a beautiful flush to her face. Her tears animated her eyes, making them almost sparkle.

"You know why, babygirl." His voice was low and even.

"I don't! I don't!"

Logan picked up his leather belt. Taking a step back he admired her lithe form, petite yet curvy. Her slim thighs ended with the glorious curve of her ass. Her waist nipped in to accentuate the soft lines of her back. Sleek brown hair, straight till it curled at the edges, hung down past her shoulders. As she struggled against her T-shirt bind, he caught glimpses of her perky tits when her body twisted and turned.

Grabbing the long shaft of his cock through his jeans, he gave the rigid length a squeeze to ease the tension.

Flexing the belt a few times to warm up the leather, he folded it in half, the buckle dangling just below his wrist. Measuring its weight, he placed a restraining hand between her shoulder blades.

"I know all about you, Chloe. You need this more than even you know."

He raised his arm and swung it sharply forward, catching her bare backside with the smooth, wide side of his belt. The contact of leather and skin made a deep, cracking noise.

Chloe screeched in pain as her hips swung sharply to the right.

Ignoring her cries, Logan cracked the leather on her ass a second time. "Your whole life you've acted without thought to consequence. Wild. Lacking discipline."

The leather belt fell across her cheeks a third time. Her pale skin began to blotch a mottled red. He watched as she clenched her bottom cheeks against the pain only to release them the moment she realized that caused more agony to her burning skin.

"Getting yourself into all kinds of trouble. More trouble than you realize this time."

He whipped her bottom again. This time the strap fell just below her cheeks to catch her upper thighs. An angry red stripe appeared on her flesh. Her howls of pain bounced off the wall.

"What you need, babygirl, is someone to keep you in line."

The metal of the heavy belt buckle jangled as he increased his pace, peppering her bottom with leather swats.

"Someone to teach you it is dangerous to lie."

"Stop! Stop! Please! I'll tell you the truth! Please just stop!" she sobbed.

"Beg me."

"Please! Please, stop." She sniffed loudly as he watched the tears course down her bright red cheeks. Flushed with pain, they almost matched the crimson blush on her bottom.

Black eyelashes fluttered over dark gray eyes glazed with pain.

Logan knew the pain from her punishment clouded her thoughts. He stroked his knuckles down her cheek with the hand that held the belt. Lowering his hand, he let the smooth, warm leather of his belt slide along her delicate flesh. Tracing the path of her tears.

Her lower lip trembled.

He raised his arm.

"No!" Her eyes were wide with obvious alarm. "Please, please, stop."

His cock twitched the moment the forced plea left her lips. Logan wasn't sure where his demand had even come from. It just felt right with Chloe. All the while he had been researching her, learning about her, studying her as a means to get to Chad to find what he had been hired to recover…one prevailing thought kept coming to the fore. If ever there was a girl who needed direction in her life, some discipline, it was her.

His babygirl.

"Good girl. Now you're going to tell me where Chad is, aren't you?" He placed a threatening hand on her left bottom cheek. Splaying his fingers, he rubbed her heated skin in deceptively soothing circles.

"I can't," she whined.

"You don't want to make me angry again do you, babygirl? Because I can get a lot meaner."

"Please, you don't understand."

"Tell me." His dug the tips of his fingers into the soft flesh of her bottom, squeezing hard. She rose up on her toes in a futile effort to escape his grip as he watched her flesh go from crimson to white from the pressure of his hand.

"All right! All right!" she gasped.

He loosened his grip.

"He's dead. I… I killed him."

His very bad babygirl.

CHAPTER 5

Chloe screwed her eyes shut, bracing for the lash of his leather belt at her admission.

None came.

She opened her eyes and turned her head to look over her shoulder. Chloe saw her tormentor through a prism of tears. He looked fearsome standing there in his torn jeans and tight white T-shirt. The dark ink of his tattoos peeked through the thin fabric, an ominous staccato across his tanned skin. In his fist was the folded leather belt.

She turned her head back around and pressed her forehead against the wall. Never in her life had she felt such a storm of conflicting emotions. Her body sagged a bit as her knees started to buckle. This evening she had run the gamut of emotions. To think, just a few hours ago she had been regretting how boring and humdrum her life had become since sequestering herself in Glennie!

Nothing made sense.

This man. This horrible, frightening man. She didn't

even know his name and yet he had already changed her in ways she could not fully fathom. The pain she felt from his punishing belt had done more than cause her physical anguish. The pain, that pure pain, had finally released her guilt. It was as if, deep down, she knew she deserved the belt and the pain...his lashing...his punishment of her. Her body had absorbed each strike of his belt like a boon. She wanted him to hurt her.

The realization caused her whole body to quake. She had wanted the pain, needed it. Then somehow it had gotten even more twisted. She not only wanted the punishing pain...she wanted the punisher as well. Wanted to feel his breath as he whispered threats into her ear. Wanted the feel of his hand on her punished ass. The feel of his teeth scraping along her skin. She could also vividly imagine his hand fisting into her hair as he forced his cock into her from behind.

What the fucking hell! What the fuck was wrong with her? This man had threatened to rape her. He still might. He now knew her to be a murderess!

She was at his mercy in more ways than she could count. How, in this moment, could her body betray her so badly? And in such a twisted, fucked up way. Had she really felt a small thrill deep between her legs the moment she'd felt the pain? Her only salvation would be if he never knew. Maybe, after learning of Chad's death, he would simply leave.

Even as she thought it, Chloe knew it was an impossibility.

Her disturbed, chaotic thoughts were interrupted by the sound of movement behind her.

The man had left the room without uttering a word.

She struggled against her wrist binds as she strained to hear what he was doing. Her view was blocked by the gun cabinet.

Chloe could hear his heavy boot-clad footfalls on the kitchen floor. He took a few steps then stopped. He was probably standing in the doorway to the study. Chad's lifeless form would be clearly visible from that viewpoint. Chloe wondered what the stranger would do now. Somehow she didn't think he was the type to call the police. Was that a good or a bad thing? Would she pray for the safety of the law and the risk of prison over whatever the stranger may have planned for her?

There was the sound of his heavy steps again.

He was returning.

"Goddamn, baby. This time you weren't lying. You actually killed the piece of shit." His words held an unmistakable hint of amusement.

Chloe continued to face the wall, whether from mortification, humiliation or guilt, she did not know. Perhaps all three?

She could hear the swish of liquid against glass.

Then came the harsh feel of denim against her sensitive, exposed skin as he pressed his front to her back. His breath smelled of whiskey as he spoke. "Did you enjoy killing him, baby? Did you like the power, the rush that comes from taking another human being's life?"

She felt the cold tip of what must have been the whiskey bottle press between her shoulder blades. The same whiskey she had used to kill Chad.

"How did you do it?"

The lip of the bottle moved downward. A sick caress.

"Did you hit him over the head?"

The bottle lip tapped against her lower back.

"No? Stab him?"

The glass lip slid over the curve of her right buttock, cold against her hot skin.

"No? Poison then? The choice of clever women for hundreds of years." The tone of his voice was darkly seductive, teasing, belying the evil of his words.

Chloe sucked in a gasp as the lip of the bottle pushed between her legs, just under the curve of her ass. She pressed her legs together tightly in defiance. He forced the glass lip past her resistance. The neck of the bottle wedged between her thighs.

"Tell me, babygirl," he whispered against her ear before giving her neck a quick lick with his tongue. "Tell me how you killed the bad man."

Chloe cried out when she felt the bottle shift. The bottle lip pressed against her tight entrance. Her wet pussy offered no resistance to the smooth glass. The neck of the bottle slid inside her... one inch... then two.

A moan escaped through her clenched teeth.

The man gave a low, soft whistle. "Goddamn, I knew I was right about you."

Chloe felt a hot tear escape down the side of her cheek. Right about her? That she was a murderess? That she was a freak who apparently got off on pain? She wasn't sure what he meant and had absolutely no intention of asking him.

The bottle twisted inside of her. Chloe cried out, but

not from pain. Despite her intention not to, she begged him. "Take it out." Her voice was hoarse from crying.

"You know how I like to be asked," he responded as he gave the bottle another twist.

Chloe moaned. The friction inside her pussy as it stretched around the bottle neck was too much after the chaos of the feelings his punishment had inspired. Without hesitation, she answered, desperate to end her torment. "*Please*, take it out."

He chuckled. "Good girl."

The bottle was pulled free.

Chloe could not help but look at him over her shoulder. She watched in fascinated horror as he lifted the bottle to his full lips. Giving her a wink, he wrapped his lips around the tip and took a swig of whiskey. "Even better tasting," he said as he gave her another wink with one of those deep blue eyes.

Her only response was a helpless whimper.

* * *

"Now, you stay here like a good babygirl while I go and clean up your mess."

Chloe gritted her teeth at his patronizing tone. As if she had a choice! He had released her bound wrists only to drag her into the bathroom. There he'd handcuffed her to the radiator. Handcuffed! What kind of man carried handcuffs around with him? The kind who had neck tattoos and punished complete strangers with their belt, apparently.

"Are you going to call the cops on me?"

"Why would I do that?"

Chloe stared at him in confusion. "Because I killed a man."

The stranger shrugged his shoulders. "Happens," he responded dismissively. "Besides, if I call the cops, they will drag you away to prison, and I'm not finished with you yet."

With those ominous words, the stranger turned to leave.

"What is your name?" she called after him. "You can at least tell me your name."

He turned back to her, piercing her with those brilliantly blue eyes of his. "Logan," he said simply. Then he leaned forward, caging her in between two muscular arms before straightening up and exiting the bathroom.

A few minutes later, she could hear the unmistakable sounds of a body being dragged across the floor, then the slamming of her back screen door.

Then nothing.

Silence.

Chloe looked down at her wrinkled, filthy T-shirt. It barely reached to the top of her thighs and was her only covering. She shifted her position on the floor, grimacing as the movement caused her still-sore bottom to ache.

The bastard had actually *spanked* her with his belt! Chloe was not sure what was worse, the fact that he had violated her that way, or the fact that her body liked it.

She then looked longingly at her glass-enclosed shower. She supposed she should be thinking about Chad right now. She *had* just killed him. Truth be told, she couldn't muster up even a tiny damn for the sick bastard.

If she hadn't killed him, he would have killed her for sure. She refused to allow him to fuck up her life any more than he already had by wallowing in remorse or shame or some misplaced Catholic guilt over ending his life. He had caused misery and death and would have continued to do so to others, of that she had no doubt. No, she wouldn't waste a single tear or a moment's regret on killing Chad.

Besides, there was her current predicament to tackle. Logan obviously was here for the same thing Chad had been ranting about, but for the life of her, she didn't know what they were referring to. Even if she did, she sure as fuck wouldn't tell Logan. It could be her only ticket out of this mess. Her only bargaining chip.

Leverage.

That is if she could figure out what the fuck *it* was first.

Chad had started with the bookshelves in the study. Was it a piece of paper? A book? Drugs? Obviously he'd thought it was something she had found and hidden somewhere in the cabin. That could only mean one thing; it was something she had taken with her from Louisiana. She hadn't completely lied to Chad. There were still a few small boxes she hadn't unpacked. They just weren't in the bedroom closet like she had told him. They were tucked away in the garage. She needed to search those boxes, but how? She couldn't just go rummaging about; Logan would find her and immediately guess what she was doing.

If she escaped, Logan would tear apart the cabin and the garage, and probably find whatever it was that Chad

had been looking for. If she stayed and risked searching herself, Logan would catch her, of that she was certain.

Did she dare try to kill him? Chloe dismissed the idea immediately. She suspected that Logan's soul might be just as stained as Chad's, but there was something about him...no...she couldn't kill him.

At least not yet. She would try to get away to search the boxes first. There was another gun cabinet in the garage. Before she searched, she would arm herself. If Logan found her searching, well, she would do whatever she had to in order to survive.

All that could wait. Right now, all she really wanted was a shower and her bed. This night had strained her nerves taut. She needed time. Time to lick her wounds and regroup. Time to think up a plan.

Too bad she was helplessly chained to her own radiator!

* * *

"You're welcome."

Chloe came awake with a start then groaned as her neck wrenched. She had fallen asleep on the floor, leaning awkwardly against the wall.

"What?" she asked dazedly.

"I said, you're welcome."

Chloe focused on Logan. His massive form dwarfed the small bathroom. He was covered in mud from the swipe on his cheek to his caked boots. He still looked hot as fuck. Damn him! She was going straight to hell and not just for being a murderer. There was just something about the raw power of his muscled form. His command of the situation. His dominance over her.

This was sick. Wrong. This man was holding her captive in her own home. He was mean and dangerous. She needed to get the fuck away from him, not admire how he looked covered in dirt!

Logan stepped forward till his legs were straddling her outstretched ones. From her position on the floor, she had a very clear view of his jeans. The hard outline of his cock was clearly marked as it sloped down the inside of his right thigh. *Holy fuck.*

As he stared down at her prone form, Logan reached for the hem of his dirty T-shirt. Pulling it over his head, he exposed his chest and chiseled abs to her gaze. Her mouth fell open at the display of ink. The tattoo she'd glimpsed on his neck was actually the handle of a dagger. The rest of the tattoo covered his shoulder and right pec. It was a wicked-looking blade piercing a red rose. On his other shoulder was the ace of spades and the queen of hearts. Along his left hipbone were the initials E.W.M.N. Chloe remembered from some random documentary she had watched that that was a prison tattoo. It stood for evil, wicked, mean and nasty. *Holy fuck.*

His large hands then went to the button on his jeans as he took a step back to kick off his boots.

"What are you doing?" she asked, alarmed.

"Undressing. Burying a guy in the woods tends to be a messy business. I need a shower." His lips twisted into a smirk.

Chloe rattled the handcuffs against the iron of the old radiator. "Then unlock me first."

"Why, babygirl. You want to join me?" He gave her a knowing wink.

Her cheeks burned with mortification both at his suggestion and the truth of his words. Honestly, she needed help…serious help.

"Absolutely not!" she responded through clenched teeth as she crossed her legs and raised her knees protectively up to her chest.

"Then you stay where you are."

He flicked open the brass buttons at his crotch. The jeans slid off his hips and fell to his ankles. Of course he would be the type to go commando, she thought sardonically. She turned her head sharply to the left and closed her eyes.

"Look at me, baby."

Chloe shook her head no.

"I said, look at me."

Chloe still shook her head no.

She heard a resigned sigh. "Does someone need to feel the strap of my belt again so soon?"

Chloe gasped in shock as she quickly whipped her head forward. She was met by the sight of his cock jutting proudly from between his legs. The huge, bulbous head looked threatening. The sheer length and girth of his shaft was intimidating to say the least. She could not look away as he fisted it. His long fingers wrapped around the thick shaft, his hand pumping along its length.

The small room slowly filled with steam. She could feel the heavy, warm air against her cheeks and lips. Without thought, the tip of her tongue swiped the moisture from her lower lip.

She watched his eyes darken as his grip tightened on his cock. Was it her fevered imagination, or had an animal growl just rumbled from deep inside his chest?

Without a word, Logan turned his back on her and stepped into the hot stream of water, but not before she'd gotten a glimpse of a large back tattoo which stretched over each shoulder blade. They were a pair of black angel wings.

Dear God.

Knowing it was pointless, she still pulled on her wrist, testing the strength of the handcuffs. Her heart racing, she felt like a trapped animal. Prey to the beast lurking behind that sheer pane of thin glass.

She watched in horrified fascination as he showered. His body was heavy with muscle. Thick arms and a wide back with narrow hips and powerful legs. He had that cut-in look over his hipbones that you usually only saw on athletes.

There were also scars. Lots of them.

There were angry red slashes and one star-shaped scar that looked suspiciously like a bullet hole just below his left ribcage.

The shower door glass fogged over, but she could still see his form. Could see him grab her body wash. Watched as he lathered the creamy soap between his strong hands. Then he began to spread it over his chest in large, sweeping circles. The room filled with the warm scent of vanilla and shea butter. As he stood to the side, she could see the outline of his cock. Watched as his soapy hand gripped it again and swept up and down, up and down.

Chloe forced her gaze away. Her eyes fell to his mud-splattered jeans on the floor. There was the edge of what looked like a photograph poking out from the back pocket. Hazarding a careful glance towards the shower and seeing that his back was turned, she risked leaning over and giving the photo a tug so she could see the full image. She was shocked to see her own face staring back at her. Her hair was much longer. The photograph had to be at least three years old. How had he gotten it? The only explanation was he must have found it on one of her old social media sites even though she'd thought she'd deleted them all when she'd fled Louisiana. Earlier, when he'd said he knew all about her, Chloe had assumed that had just been a threat to scare her into obeying. Now, she was not so sure.

Who the hell was this guy?

Her attention returned to Logan as she shoved the photo back into his pocket. He rinsed off the suds and opened the door, but left the shower running.

Walking over to her still-prone form, heedless of his own nakedness, Logan crouched down. With a wicked grin, he said, "Your turn."

Chloe shook her head as she once again tucked her knees up to her chest. "No. I... I don't want a shower."

Logan reached out and flicked the tip of her nose. If it hadn't been for the fact that he was her captor, she would have thought it an affectionate gesture.

"This isn't about what you want."

Logan dug through his jeans pocket for the handcuff key. The moment her right hand was freed, Chloe took a swing at him. It would not be as effective as the first time;

he had deliberately removed her amethyst ring before locking her up. But she still had to try.

Logan snagged her wrist before she made contact with his jaw. Grabbing her other wrist, he effortlessly pulled her up off the floor.

"I just love when you fight me," he taunted. Fisting the limp collar of her T-shirt, he viciously tore downward, tearing her only garment off her before forcing both of her arms behind her back.

"Go to hell," she snarled as she twisted her shoulders, trying to break free of his hold.

There was a loud metallic snap. Both her wrists were secured behind her. Chloe was once again helpless to fight him.

"Time for your bath, babygirl."

Wrapping a possessive arm around her waist, he pressed her body against his own as he lifted her off the floor and carried her into the shower. The heat of the water as it hit her face and chest momentarily stole her breath. Chloe shook her head as wet strands of hair covered her eyes.

Logan pressed her against the tile wall of the shower as his large palm brushed her wet curls back. Moving his hand down, he cupped her jaw. His thumb swept over her lower lip as he stared at her mouth.

The pain in her arms from being trapped between her body and the wall was nothing compared to the torment of the emotions having his hard body pressed against her own caused.

"Please," she whimpered. The fight in her gone.

He swiped her lower lip with his thumb again. "I like

the sound of you begging me." He continued to stare at her mouth, a look of concentrated fascination animating his sharp features. "Usually, I study a target's eyes. You can learn a lot from just looking at the eyes. Not with you. It was your mouth. This sweet, pink mouth. Photo after photo. The way your plump lower lip would pout when it was obvious you didn't want your photo taken. The cute cupid bow of your top lip. How you rarely wear lipstick, never covering up the natural blush pink of your lips. I began to wonder how they would look after I forced my cock into your tight, tiny mouth. Would they be swollen? Bitten? Would they blush a darker pink?"

Chloe couldn't move. The heat of the shower as the water pounded against her skin and the feel of his hard cock pushing against her stomach. The sensual threat of his words as he continued to stroke her lower lip, then pressed the tip of his thumb against her teeth. It all held her motionless.

"Why am I a target? I've done nothing to you. I don't even know you!"

"But I know you. That was very clever, what you did with Internal Affairs. The feigned innocence. Those idiot detectives didn't suspect for a moment you were leading them around by the nose. They didn't even know you had given them a fake name. Tell me. How long did it take you to plan your boyfriend's demise? A week? A few days?"

Chloe felt sick. How could he possibly know that? It was how she had managed to slip out of Louisiana and never be tracked down for Chad's trial as a witness. She had created a fake persona, complete with social media profiles and fake I.D. She had always wondered why Chad

had never ratted her out. She now knew it was because she was in possession of something he didn't want the cops to find...something he had planned all along to retrieve. Still, that didn't explain how Logan had learned of her subterfuge. She had told no one. She had no one to tell.

"How... how do you know about that?"

Logan ran his finger over her collarbone. He then caressed the soft curve of her breast before circling the pert nipple.

"Let's just say I get paid very well by some very powerful people to learn secrets, to find what's hidden, to clean up messes. And you, babygirl, are all three."

Chloe's lower lip trembled with fear. She had a thousand questions, none of which she suspected he would answer. Still, she had to ask one. "Are you going to kill me?"

She could feel his hand pressing against the delicate ribs of her ribcage before sliding over her wet skin to her hip. He then flipped his hand to run his knuckles over her flat abdomen, barely skimming over the neatly trimmed, soft brown curls covering her pussy.

She swallowed a gasp when he possessively cupped her mound, forcing his middle finger between her lower lips. "That depends. Are you going to be a good girl and tell me what I want to know?"

"I don't know what Chad was looking for!"

"You're lying."

He slid an arm around her waist to wrap around her lower back, forcing her chest forward and relieving the pressure on her arms. Pushing his middle finger into her cunt, he said, "The more you insist on lying to me, the harder I will make this on you. I *will* get what I want. Whether you survive the effort is up to you."

With those words, he ruthlessly pushed a second finger into her tight heat. Chloe cried out as she arched up onto her toes. It had been years since she had been touched, and even then her only experience was Chad's inept fumblings. This was... this was... oh God! Her body clenched around his thrusting fingers, pulling him in deeper.

Logan's free hand slipped down to grasp her left bottom cheek as he curled the tip of his fingers inside of her, brushing the sensitive hidden nerves.

Her head fell back as she let out a tortured moan.

"Ask me to let you come."

She opened lust-glazed eyes, forcing herself to focus on his words. "I... I...."

He dug his fingers into her still-sore bottom. "Beg me like a good girl."

She couldn't. Her body might be betraying her, but she still needed to fight him. Fight this strange power he seemed to have over her.

He shifted his feet and opened his legs wider, the press of his cock against her hip more insistent as his hand moved faster, thrusting his fingers into her tight hole. His other hand moved along her slick skin. She felt his fingertips press into the cleft of her bottom.

Chloe's eyes widened in alarm. "No!"

She jerked her hips forward to avoid his touch, but that simply pressed her body more closely to his.

He smiled. "Yes." His fingers pushed between her

cheeks. The tip of his index finger caressing the soft, puckered skin of her bottom hole.

Chloe clenched against his touch.

He forced the tip past her resistance. Pushed his thick index finger into her bottom past the first knuckle.

Her protest was garbled as she struggled to come to terms with the assault on such an intimate, heretofore untouched, part of her body.

Logan leaned down and bit her plump lower lip.

She tasted the metallic tang of blood on her tongue just as he pushed those two fingers back inside her pussy and the finger inside her bottom deeper, caressing the thin layer of skin separating the two passages.

The taste of blood. The feeling of powerlessness, of being dominated, forced. It was primal. Fierce. Overwhelming. But most of all, frighteningly liberating.

"Beg me," he commanded.

"Please! Please make me come!" she shouted in defeat, her body winning out over her will.

Pressed so close, she could feel the vibrations of his growl from deep within his chest as he worked both hands in a powerful rhythm. Chloe screamed her release as her body fell limp in his arms.

Spent. Defeated.

She kept her eyes closed as he released his grip and propped her against the warmed tiles. She smelled vanilla and shea butter moments before she felt his hands on her shoulders. He massaged the soap into her skin with long, sweeping circles. Over her breasts, stomach, down her thighs…and between. She was lifted against his hard length as he pulled them both fully under the stream of hot water. His fingers delved into her thick curls as he shampooed her hair, massaging her neck and scalp. Once again, his gestures and touch were almost affectionate.

The deliberate switch between forceful and gentle kept her on edge and off-balance.

After rinsing her hair, he fisted her locks and pulled her head back. She felt his body shift as he leaned in close to whisper into her ear, "Time for your punishment, babygirl."

CHAPTER 6

He really was a sick bastard. With any other target, he would have put a gun to their head to force them to talk, then retrieved the package and been long gone. There was just something about Chloe. She was an intoxicating contradiction, both wicked and innocent. Clever as a whip, she had managed to outwit an entire division of detectives and escape with a package worth more to his client than all the cocaine in New Orleans. From the moment he had started tracking her, learning about her, he had been intrigued. A brutal childhood, a dick for a boyfriend, no education beyond high school; any combination of those three would have been enough to drive an ordinary woman into the gutter. Drugs, drink, prostitution, pick your poison.

But not his Chloe. His Chloe. Yeah, she was his now. He had claimed her before he had even set eyes on her.

Despite the brutality of her early life, she'd chosen a career creating beautiful objects. She collected dolls. Her

Netflix account was filled with G- and PG-rated movies. She wore Hello Kitty panties. Yet, despite the delight she took in innocent pursuits, there was still a restless darkness lurking behind her eyes. A darkness that called to him. He wanted to see that darkness, to taste it on her tongue, to feel her tremble with it as he pushed his cock inside her. He wanted it all...every bit of her. The innocence and the darkness. He wanted to be the one to possess her, to dominate her...to break her. To bring out her demons, so she would have no choice but to turn to him for protection from the very monsters he created inside her soul.

Yeah, he was a sick bastard, but he had no intention of relenting. Her fate had been sealed from the moment she'd become his target. His prey. He was enjoying this too much to stop now.

Tilting her chin back, he looked into her large, confused eyes. "You didn't think I would forget that you lied to me again?"

Her eyes lowered, trying to shut him out. It was no use. He was already in.

Placing his hands on her slim shoulders, he pushed down, forcing her to her knees. His back blocked the worst of the shower stream from hitting her in the face, but droplets still formed on her eyelashes and cheeks.

"Haven't you humiliated me enough?"

"Oh, I've only just begun."

Fisting his cock, he rubbed the bulbous tip along her lower lip. "Say you want to suck my cock."

Her eyes narrowed as she shot him a stubborn glare.

Using his free hand to fist her hair, he repeated his command.

"I want to suck your cock," she said. Her jaw clenched tight. The words barely audible.

He gave her wet locks a sharp tug.

Getting his silent message, she reluctantly repeated, "Please, I want to suck your cock."

Taking a step closer till his feet were pressed in on either side of her thighs, Logan tilted his cock upwards, rubbing the sensitive underside against the cute tip of her nose.

"Does it make you feel like a dirty girl when I make you say such dirty things?"

He could not tell if it was tears or water droplets that streamed down her cheeks. Her face was so beautifully expressive. He could see her struggling. Struggling to fight her response to his rough handling.

"Yes," she whispered. He could barely hear her over the rush of the shower.

"Louder. Tell me how your cunt clenched when I forced you to your knees. How, deep down, you want me to force those lying lips of yours open. Force you to accept my cock."

"Please don't make me," she whimpered.

"Say it," he ordered. "Say please force your cock down my throat."

He waited, watching her eyes closely. Watching the storm in their dark gray depths. Watching as the darkness clouded them over.

"Please force your cock down my throat."

"Good girl. Now open up."

He pushed the head of his cock past her lips, groaning when he felt the slight sharp edge of her teeth on the underside. He watched her struggle as he pushed deeper. Her lips stretched thin around the thick shaft. He felt the kiss of air on his cock as she tried to suck in a breath from the corners of her mouth. Pushing his fingers into her wet hair, he applied steady pressure to the back of her head.

"That's it, babygirl. Open your throat up. Open it. Take it down, nice and slow."

Ignoring her chokes and gasps, he thrust his hips forward. Closing his eyes, he savored the sense of absolute power as the tip of his cock pushed against the back of her tight throat. With her hands still handcuffed behind her back, she was completely at his mercy. Putting more pressure on the back of her head, he forced her to swallow another two inches till he could feel the tip of her nose touch his abdomen. She started to struggle. From his vantage point, he could see her fingers spasm and clench as she pulled against the metallic manacles on her wrists, desperate to free her hands so she could push him off.

Gripping her hair, he pulled her off his cock, tilting her head back as he leaned down. "What are you doing right now, baby?"

She didn't hesitate. "Sucking your cock."

"You want me to punish you for being a bad girl? You want me to choke you with my cock? Force it deep?"

"Yes, choke me. Make me pay. Make it hurt."

Both hands holding either side of her face, he pushed his cock back in. This time thrusting his hips. Using her mouth. Instinctively knowing she needed this punishment. Needed him to punish her. Needed the pain.

They both needed it.

As he felt his balls tighten, Logan ground out, "Swallow every fucking drop of my come," before he shot it down her throat with a roar.

* * *

AFTER REMOVING THE HANDCUFFS, he dried her off and wrapped her snugly in a large towel. Lifting her into his arms, Logan carried her into the bedroom. Without asking her opinion, he searched through her closet as she sat motionless on the bed. He found pink adult footie pajamas with cute rabbit ears on the hoodie. Unwrapping the towel, he knelt in front of her to place her feet in them.

"Wait. I need panties." Her voice was soft and small-sounding.

"No you don't." He pulled the pajamas up over her legs. "Scoot that cute ass of yours up."

He was pleased to see her obey without argument. Taking one last look at her full breasts, he zipped her pajamas up. Once again, he gathered her into his arms and carried her into the kitchen. Sitting her on a stool at the island, he admonished, "One false move and I will strip off those jammies and force you to sit there naked and handcuffed. You understand, baby?"

She nodded.

Damn she looked adorable. Her cheeks were still

flushed from her punishment. Her eyes large and bright. All cuddled up in pink fuzzy fabric.

Tearing his gaze away, he opened the fridge. He hadn't eaten since yesterday, and he was fairly certain she had missed her dinner.

"Seriously? All you have in here are old Chinese food containers. There isn't a single vegetable or even a carton of milk." He opened the freezer. Pulling out the sole bag he found there, he turned a sardonic look on her. "Frozen chicken nuggets. All you have in your freezer is a single bag of frozen chicken nuggets. This is no way to eat, baby."

Chloe shrugged her shoulders. "I don't really cook."

He felt it again. A strange tug-of-war inside his chest. A dual need to both punish and protect her.

Logan pulled out a carton of eggs, some butter and a packet of cheese he found in the crisper. After rooting around for a pan, he set to work making them omelets.

"Are you going to tell me who you are working for?"

"No."

"Will you tell me how I became a target?"

"You already know how. You have something they want. I've been hired to get it back...by any means necessary."

"So this... all... this.... is you just messing with me until I tell you what you want to know? Until your client gets back whatever Chad was looking for."

He could hear the vulnerability in her voice. For a moment, he thought about lying to her, telling her it was all just a game to break her, but that was not how he operated. He was always straight with people. Even people he killed. He never lied about his intentions. It wasted his time and just added insult to injury.

"No. Trust me, baby. This is no game. Whether you asked for it or not, you are caught up in a dangerous mess."

As he flipped the omelets, he hazarded a glance over his shoulder. She was pulling on the cuffs of her pajamas, averting her eyes.

"You could always just leave. Tell them you couldn't find me. Couldn't find it."

He pulled two plates down from the cupboard and plated the omelets. "Can't do that."

She turned pleading eyes up to him. "Why not?"

"Because I always find my targets. Because I've never not finished a job. Because if it wasn't me, they'd send someone worse."

"Worse than you?" she brazenly quipped.

He set a plate and fork in front of her. Spearing a piece of omelet with his fork, he laughed. "Hell yeah. They could send someone with a smaller cock who couldn't cook." He gave her a seductive wink before opening his mouth and swallowing a buttery bite of egg.

She pushed the omelet around her plate. Finally, she said in a hesitant voice, "I really don't know what you're looking for, and you don't seem inclined to tell me whatever it is anyway. I doubt it's here. I didn't take anything of Chad's with me when I left Louisiana."

"I know."

Her fork clattered as she dropped it on the plate. She threw up her arms in disgust. "Then why? Why are you holding me captive? Why are you punishing me? Why don't you just leave?"

He walked around the island till he faced her. Placing one arm around her back and the other under her knees, he picked her up. Switching positions, he sat on the high-backed stool and settled her on his lap. Picking up the fork, he cut off a piece of her untouched omelet. Holding it up to her lips, he smiled when she stubbornly turned her face away. "Open your mouth, or I will put you back on your knees and give you something else to swallow."

Her cheeks burned a brighter shade of pink as she reluctantly turned and opened her mouth, allowing him to feed her.

"I am holding you captive because, while I believe you don't know what it is my client is after, I don't believe you don't know where it might be."

Chloe averted her eyes.

He took hold of her chin to force her to face him again. Applying a small amount of pressure to her jaw, he persuaded her to open her mouth to receive another bite.

Yeah, he could definitely get used to this, he thought as his cock began to swell from the pressure of her bottom on his lap and the sight of her opening her mouth to receive food from him.

"I'm punishing you because, not only do you deserve it, you want it. You like the pain. You like when I bend you to my will. Face it, baby. You are a dark and twisted soul. You killed a man without batting one pretty eyelash, but that kind of coldness leaves a black mark. It's a dark energy that swirls inside you, destroying you if you don't let it out. You need to give it an outlet. I'm that outlet for you. I'm both your demon and your demon slayer, and I'm not leaving because I'm not finished with you yet."

From her position nestled on his lap, he could feel her body shiver from his words.

"Now. How do you thank me for making dinner?"

"Thank you," she said with only slightly feigned sweetness.

CHAPTER 7

"You're the ones who created this fucking mess, so don't dictate to me how I clean it up. It wasn't my idea to help Chad escape prison only to lose track of him. The girl is your only option, and I won't be questioned in how I deal with her. You'll have your package in a few days."

Chloe sat up in bed. Logan must be talking to whoever had made her a target. His client.

She wrapped her arms around her middle. The cozy warmth of the bed faded away as cold reality crept in. She had only a hazy memory of being put to bed. Having some food in her stomach and the strange impression of feeling safe in Logan's arms had chased away the early horrors of the day and lulled her into a restful sleep. She remembered the sensation of being lifted in his arms and carried, then the soft comfort of a blanket. Chloe looked to her right. There was an unmistakable dent in the other pillow. He must have slept next to her. The thought made her blush.

"You send more men and I'll fucking offer the package out to the highest bidder." His deep voice penetrated through the heavy oak bedroom door.

Her cheeks burned hotter at her momentary folly. He was her captor. She was a job to him, a paycheck. Any affection he showed her was probably all a part of his game. There was still no guarantee he wouldn't kill her once he found what his client wanted. Her only chance was to find it first.

Chloe crept from the bed. Hiding herself in her closet, she quickly changed out of the fuzzy pink novelty pajamas and into some yoga pants and a hoodie. Slipping on a pair of pink Converse sneakers, she silently walked across the bedroom to the sliding door which led to the back porch. Grimacing at the scraping sound as the door eased open, she cast a furtive glance at the closed bedroom door…and waited. After the span of several heartbeats, she heard his voice again.

"I'm through talking with you. Put Michaels on the phone. Then go find him."

The anger in his voice was evident. Good. The louder he yelled, the less likely it was he would hear her movements.

Leaving the door ajar, she carefully made her way over the still-damp boards of the back porch, not sparing a glance for her favorite view of the lake. Its ducks and geese would do nothing to calm her nerves now. She came upon the second glass sliding door. This one led to the living room which had a view into the kitchen.

If he walked into the living room, he would see her pass.

She could either run past and hope he wasn't in the room, or risk peeking. Chloe was breathing so hard she felt lightheaded. Fisting her shaking hands at her sides, she leaned over and hazarded a quick glance through the glass.

The room was empty.

Not wasting any more time, she scurried past and made her way down the rickety steps and across the leaf-strewn yard toward the garage.

Once inside, she ran past the neat rows of white cabinets to the tall gun safe in the corner. Punching in the code, she wrenched open the heavy door. Inside was her own S&W Ladysmith .38 special. Checking to make sure it was loaded, she tucked the gun into her front hoodie pocket. Its heavy weight was both comforting and disturbing.

The boxes. Those damn boxes. Where had she put them?

Turning in harried circles, she tried to think. It would be only a matter of minutes before Logan discovered her gone. She needed to figure out where and what the package was and hide it before then.

It was her only chance at leverage.

Remembering the empty cabinet in the far-left corner, Chloe ran over and pulled on its plastic handle. There inside were the two small boxes she had brought with her from Louisiana. Pulling them out, she crouched down and tore at the old shipping tape. Opening the first, she rummaged through the contents. A few old CDs, a tiny canvas depicting Jackson Square which she had gotten from a local artist in happier times, and an ugly doll Chad

had given her. It was a wretched, pathetic-looking thing, with glued-on hair and a head that looked like it had been ripped off the body of another doll. He had said something about it belonging to a dead relative, so she would have felt guilty about just throwing it away. She was intent on opening the second box when someone cleared their throat.

Scrambling up and taking a shocked step backwards, she stared into Logan's shuttered blue eyes. His feet were bare. Faded jeans hung low on his hips, the top button undone. His chest was also bare, displaying the ink she found so fascinating and the scars that made her wonder what kind of life he'd led. The cheeks of his unshaven jaw curled up from the smirk lingering on his full lips as he lounged against the doorjamb. The dark smell of coffee from the mug in his hand filled the small room.

"I'm beginning to think you don't like me," he quipped.

Chloe was silent.

She watched as his eyes fell on the open boxes at her feet.

"I knew you would lead me to the package eventually."

Chloe pulled the gun from her hoodie pocket. "Stay back," she warned.

Logan didn't move. He stood there and smiled. *The bastard smiled!*

"That's my girl. Always full of fight and fire."

"I'm not your girl. You're... you're too late anyway. I already found it and destroyed it."

"You forget, babygirl. I always know when you are lying to me." Logan straightened and took a step toward her.

"I mean it. I'll shoot."

He placed his mug down on a nearby workbench and crossed his arms over his chest. "No, baby, you won't. You may have killed, but you're not a killer."

Chloe's outstretched arm faltered. "You only think you know me."

"I know you are alone and in way over your head. I know you won't survive this mess without me."

Chloe bit her lip in indecision.

He took another step closer. "I know you did everything in your power to stop Chad from hurting that boy and his father. I know you are punishing yourself with guilt."

No longer questioning how he knew such details about her past, about her, Chloe blurted out, "He just started beating on him. I don't know why. I… I'd always justified things he'd done before because he did them to thugs and gang members, but this was just an ordinary, innocent family." Chloe sniffed as tears formed in her eyes. Her guilt over her past loosened her tongue. "After that, I just couldn't take it anymore. I had to escape."

"The father wasn't innocent. He laundered money for a powerful Columbian gang. The fucker got greedy. Over the course of a year, he slowly moved around fifteen million out of their accounts into new unknown ones. The new account numbers and passwords were stored on a small flash drive. The gang sent Chad to retrieve it, thinking the guy would fold when he saw the cop uniform. He didn't."

"Then Chad stole the flash drive?"

"Even that piece of shit wasn't that stupid. After he

killed the father and son, he went on a drug rampage. He claimed he was too high to remember where he hid it. That's what kept him alive in prison these past two years. The gang continued to protect him with the understanding he would find the drive when he got out."

"Why... why didn't they just come after me earlier?"

"They didn't know about you. Until now."

Chloe pulled the hammer back on her gun. Leveling it at his chest, she said, "You mean until you."

His features hardened as he took a threatening step forward. Forgetting she had the gun for protection, Chloe stumbled backward.

"I mean until now. Face it, baby, I'm your only protection."

Chloe tried to read his body language and expression, as if a tilt of his head or a glint in his eye would give away the truth or lie in his words. "So I'm just supposed to believe you? Believe that you were not sent by this gang to kill me?"

"If I were here to kill you, you never would have heard me coming."

The hard arrogance in his tone held an unmistakable ring of truth.

"What about the rest?"

Logan raised an eyebrow. "The rest?"

"The... the... things you made me do and say." Chloe tried and failed not to look at the distinctive bulge in his jeans. The memory of him forcing her to her knees, the taste of his cock as he'd pushed it between her lips, the satisfying sting as he'd fisted her hair, came rushing to the fore.

"You mean the punishments? The feel of my belt on that plump ass of yours? All those dirty things I made you say?" he teased, his voice dropping to a low growl.

Chloe swallowed. She could feel heat creep up her cheeks and a familiar twist in her stomach. Even now his dominant stance, the swagger in his tone, how he seemed to command the situation even though she was the one with the gun.... It all fucked with her thoughts, confusing her about how she should be feeling toward him. Her only response was a jerky nod.

"Because you are a beautiful fucked up mess. You have a sweet candy coating that hides all your dark and twisted thoughts. I'm the best at what I do because I know people, and baby, you may not like it, but you need the punishment, the fear, the lack of control. You need to feel the pain of punishment in order to earn the pleasure of the reward. You need a strong man in your life. Someone to both punish and protect you."

"Who says you're the man for the job? Maybe I have someone else in my life." Chloe didn't know why she felt the need to taunt the beast. The truth of his words had cut a little too close to the bone. She needed to distance herself from him.

Like a fierce animal, he bared his teeth and actually growled at her. "If there was, he would be dead by now."

Unsure how to respond to such an overwhelmingly possessive statement, she asked, "So what happens now?"

Logan smiled, the expression failing to reach his eyes. "Now, you have a choice. If you don't want this, you had better pull that trigger, otherwise I am through with talking."

Holy fuck! He was right. She must be dark and twisty if that did it for her. The thought of this powerful man directing all his intense energy at her made her melt. She wanted the feel of his hand on her ass. She wanted to be pushed against a wall and fucked. She wanted to taste each and every one of his tattoos and kiss each scar. She wanted the danger, the pain.

Logan scared her to death, but she had never felt more alive. If trusting him was a mistake…well, she had made far worse in her life.

Chloe took her finger off the trigger but her movements were too slow.

Logan lunged.

Pulling the gun from her now-limp grasp, he plowed forward till the force of his body crushed her against the garage's brick wall. She could feel the threatening press of his erect cock as it pushed against her stomach. His breath smelled of coffee as he moved his lips along her jaw to rasp against her open mouth, "You're mine now."

CHAPTER 8

His client was going to be pissed. Of all the ways he was expected to neutralize a situation, fucking the target was definitely not one of them. It was completely out of character for him as well. He was the cold, unfeeling bastard who cleaned up messes, got paid and moved on. Never mixing business with pleasure. Chloe was different. There was just something about the woman that had intrigued him from the beginning. Drew him in. His initial fascination had grown into something deeper and darker when he'd actually met her. A tarnished innocent. His bedeviled angel.

There would be questions later. Answers she would demand. Answers she had a right to have, but for now, he was in too deep. He was going to claim her as his own, his client and the consequences be damned.

A tremor passed through her small body as he pinned her to the wall. The impact of that slight vibration heading straight to his already hard cock.

"Say it," he growled against her lips. "Say you want me."

"Please," she moaned.

Grinding his hips against her own, he repeated his command.

"I want you," she breathed in helpless defeat.

Without another word, Logan dipped down and shouldered her midsection, easily lifting her slight weight. With an arm wrapped securely over her upper thighs, he carried his prize back to the warmth of the cabin. He dropped her on the unmade bed among the crumpled blankets and sheets. Sleeping next to her last night without touching her, without fucking her, had been torture. He had been a goddamn saint, and now he was about to get his heavenly reward. Reaching down, he pulled off both of her adorable pink sneakers. The color made him smile. He liked that her rough edges were covered in pink and glitter. There were just hints, like the Hello Kitty bra and panties, or the fuzzy footy pajamas, or the pink sneakers meant for a teenager rather than a grown woman.

"Logan, maybe we should…."

He reached down and gripped the hem of the oversized hoodie covering the top of her yoga pants. He had been annoyed that it had deprived him of a glimpse of her pert ass in these yoga pants as he'd watched her sneak across the yard into the garage. Now he would see that same ass naked and blushing red from his hand.

"Seriously, Logan. This is moving too…."

The rest of her sentence was muffled as he yanked the hoodie over her head then stripped her out of her yoga pants. He hadn't been sure in the dim lighting of the garage, but he had suspected his little minx hadn't put a bra on under the sweatshirt, and he was correct. In a matter of seconds, she was lying bare and vulnerable before him.

His hands moved to his jeans' zipper.

Chloe propped herself up on her elbows as she shifted her bottom back on the bed, all the while staring at his crotch.

"Logan, I... I'm not sure about…." She didn't get any further.

Logan grabbed her by the ankles and flipped her over onto her stomach. Raising his hand, he gave her ass two quick swats, satisfied at her cry of alarm and the bright red handprint that appeared on each cheek. As he flipped her again to her back, his faded jeans slipped past his hips and fell to his ankles. Gripping his cock, he looked down at her prone form. "Spread your legs."

After a brief hesitation, she opened her knees slightly.

Logan smiled. "I see my babygirl needs her body to be punished before her mind will allow her pleasure."

Chloe bit her lower lip, her big gray eyes wide and expressive. He could read the unspoken truth of his words in their depths.

Wrapping his hand around her slim right ankle, he pulled her leg up and out, exposing her inner thigh and cunt. Ruthlessly, he brought the full weight of his open palm down on the delicate skin of her inner thigh. Chloe howled in shock and pain as she tried in vain to twist out of his grasp. He spanked her again and again, watching her pale skin bloom to a bright, cherry red.

"Stop! Stop! Oh God. It hurts!" she screamed.

"You want me to stop?"

"Yes! Yes! You have to stop."

"Okay, baby."

He dropped her right ankle. Before she could take a breath in relief, he snatched her left ankle and yanked that leg high in the air.

"No! No! You said you would stop!" she screeched.

"I'm a man of my word, babygirl. I did stop punishing your right leg. Now it's the left's turn."

His hand began to sting from the impact as he connected with her soft skin. Slapping up and down the slim length of her inner thigh, he peppered every exposed inch.

"Stop!" Chloe cried as she began to choke on her tears.

After a few more spanks, he finally stopped. Releasing her leg, he looked her over with hooded eyes.

"Now. Are you going to spread your legs for me?"

Chloe quickly nodded her head as she opened her legs wide.

It was a gorgeous sight. Her petite form was pale against the deep blue of the blankets. The glint of moisture on the thin curls of her cunny had his mouth watering. Both of her open thighs were an angry red from the punishment she'd received at his hand.

Running a finger between the soft folds of her cunt, he said, "I'm going to feast on this pretty little cunny of yours."

Placing both knees on the bed between her outstretched legs, he ran his hands over the smooth skin of her calves. Then caressed each inner thigh, relishing in the heat radiating off her punished flesh. He placed his hands under her knees and raised them to drape her legs over his shoulders. Cupping her bottom cheeks, he lifted her hips, forcing her weight back onto her shoulders and neck. He knew it would make her feel open, exposed, completely under his control.

Loving how her warmed-up thighs felt against his face, Logan ran his tongue along the seam of her cunt. Forcing the tip between the folds, he circled her clit, applying the slightest bit of pressure with every sweep of his tongue. Increasing the pace and pressure, he had to strengthen his hold on her legs as her hips began to buck against his mouth.

"Oh God, oh God," she moaned.

"That's it, babygirl." He growled his words against the soft folds of her cunny, using the sharp abrasion from his unshaven jaw and chin to stimulate her already sensitive core.

Dropping his hands from her ass, he allowed her body to fall onto the bed. Shifting backwards, he knelt on the floor, pulling her toward him till the curve of her ass was over the edge of the bed. Sealing his open mouth fully over her clit, he licked and tasted as he placed two fingers at her cunt's tight entrance. Pushing them past her feeble resistance, he slid them in to the hilt. Rotating his wrist from side to side, he pulled his fingers free before thrusting them back into her body. Hard. Over and over, he timed the thrust of his fingers with the swirl of his tongue against her swollen clit.

Pulling his fingers free, he replaced them with the tip of his tongue, licking inside her entrance as he used both thumbs and the heels of his palms to pull her bottom cheeks apart. Her puckered hole fluttered and clenched as he blew on it. He wanted her to know his intentions before he even touched her.

"Oh! Ah… no. I, ah… I've never… please don't go… there," she stammered awkwardly.

Smiling at the fear and humiliation in her hesitant plea, Logan ran the tip of his tongue over the sensitive ridges of her forbidden hole. When it glistened from his ministrations, he replaced his tongue with the tip of his index finger. He traced the pale pink skin with the flat of his finger, teasing her.

"Please. I don't want…" she pleaded.

He watched as her cute pink-polished toes gripped the edge of the mattress in her agitation.

Without saying a word, he pushed his finger into her barely prepared ass. Twisting, he forced it straight in past the first knuckle to the base.

Chloe's hips shot off the bed. Her hands fisted in the covers as she let out a shocked yelp.

Placing his large hand on her flat abdomen, he forced her body back onto the mattress. Pulling his finger free, he thrust it back in to the hilt, relishing in how her tight hole clenched and squeezed him.

He then added a second finger. The moisture from his tongue was already gone, so this one would hurt.

"Ow! Ow! No!"

"I'll be forcing my thick cock up this tiny hole before long. You had better get used to the pain of it, baby."

Chloe whined in response.

When both fingers were inside her body, he opened

them, scissoring them as he twisted his wrist. With each movement of his hand, he would capture just the barest glimpse of the dark pink inner walls.

"Please, it hurts," she whimpered.

"Do you want me to take the pain away?"

"Yes, please!"

Running his free hand down her middle and over her cunt, he tucked two fingers against her pussy entrance.

"Tell me to fuck both holes with my fingers," he ordered.

"Please don't make me. It will hurt."

"Babygirl. What happens when you tell me no?"

She reluctantly whispered, "I get your belt."

"That's right. Now what do you say?"

He could see her chest expand as she took a deep steadying breath. "Please, fu… fuck both my holes."

With two of his fingers deep in her ass, he pushed two from his other hand inside her cunt. Curling the tips upward, he shifted his hand side to side in a deep, vibrating rhythm as he thrust his fingers in and out.

Chloe cried out. "I need your tongue. Oh God. Please!"

His lips quirked up in a knowing smile as he slowed his rhythm and leaned over her cunt, inhaling the sweet musky scent before swirling his tongue over her clit. She came almost immediately.

Her eyes were closed. Her mouth open and panting. Her upper chest and breasts flushed pink from exertion. She looked beautiful in the throes of an orgasm.

Gently pulling his fingers free, he rose up over her body. Placing a knee on the mattress, he grabbed her under the arms and shifted her body upward till she was fully on the bed. As he settled his hips between her legs, he was pleased to feel the warmed skin of her inner thighs. She was still showing the marks of his earlier punishment.

Biting her small earlobe, he growled into her ear, "My turn."

Fisting his cock, he positioned the head at her entrance. As he started to force the large, bulbous head past the clenching entrance of her pussy, her closed eyes flew open.

Pressing her hands against his chest, she tried to push him back.

"Wait. I'm not… I mean I haven't in awhile… Chad was the only…."

He clenched his jaw, tamping down the blinding red anger he felt at the mention of another man's name, let alone the name of the only man who had ever had her before him. If the man hadn't already been dead, he would probably have killed him just for touching what was now his. It didn't matter if it had been years ago.

Logan covered her mouth with his hand.

"Don't ever mention that man or any other man's name to me. Ever. I'm aware he was your first, but, baby-girl, I have every intention of being your last. You're mine, and I don't fucking share."

With that, he thrust deep, piercing her flesh with his thick shaft.

Throwing his head back, he could not prevent the primal roar which escaped as he took possession of her. She was so fucking tight. Practically virginal. His beautiful, dark angel. Now in the grasp of the devil. Already damned, he had no intentions of ever letting her go.

Pounding into her body, he lowered his head to take one perfectly ripe nipple into his mouth.

Chloe groaned and thrashed her head from side to side. "Fuck! Fuck! Harder. I'm coming!"

Her words spurred him on.

Using the sharp edges of his teeth, he rubbed them along the nub, teasing her sensitive flesh, flicking it with his tongue. He palmed her other breast, testing its weight, the soft, heavy feel of it filling his hand.

Her knees crept up to his sides as she hugged him closer into her body. Wanting the pain. Accepting each brutal thrust.

As her body clenched with her climax, he could feel his balls tighten. Using extreme discipline, he pulled free of her body. Straddling her hips, he fisted his hand in her hair, pulling her torso upright.

"Open your eyes." His dark command was harsh and insistent.

She obeyed. Her gray eyes unfocused and glazed with lust... or pain... or both.

"Good girl. I want you to see me as I mark you with my seed. Mark you as my own."

Keeping his tight grip on her hair, he fisted his cock with his free hand. Vigorously pumping his hand along the shaft, he came. He watched as his come coated her breasts, chin and lower lip.

"Lick your lips. Taste my seed."

The light pink tip of her tongue flicked out along her plump lower lip.

It wasn't enough. Not for his heated blood. Not for the primitive need still surging through his veins. Releasing his still-turgid cock, he swept his fingers along the upper curve of her breast.

Holding his come-coated fingers up to her lips, he said, "Open wide."

She opened her mouth and allowed him to feed her his come.

His sweet babygirl.

She was now completely his.

CHAPTER 9

Chloe waited till Logan left the room before flopping back on the bed and covering her eyes with her hands. *Holy fuck!* What the hell had she just gotten herself into? That old adage about getting burned when you dance with the devil came to mind. There was having a thing for bad boys and then there was getting involved with someone like Logan. The man was intense, and he played for keeps. He was also obviously *very* dangerous in more ways than one. He made Chad look like a small-time petty street thug. What the hell was she going to do now?

As she always did when she was nervous, she started to play with the small metal heart charm around her neck. It was the first piece of jewelry she had ever molded and made herself. It had both a sentimental and calming effect on her.

Did she seriously trust him to not still kill her? Yes. Deep in her gut, the answer was yes. She may be a dumb bitch, but there was something about him…a protective vibe. Admittedly, that protective vibe took the form of a strict disciplinarian, but in her own fucked up kinky way, she really liked that about him. She'd never known her father, and her mother hadn't given a rat's ass about her or her well-being. After so many years of taking care of herself and being the only one who'd given a damn whether she lived or breathed, it was intoxicating. The feeling drew her to him like a bird seeking shelter from the cold.

There was a rush of water. Logan returned.

"Up you go. Time to shower." One arm going around her shoulders and the other under her knees, he lifted her up high against his chest.

"I don't suppose you'd let me shower by myself? I do know how to wash myself you know."

His only response was a smile.

Chloe was fast learning that smile usually meant no.

* * *

CHLOE WAS FINALLY ALONE, toweling off in the bathroom. The moment the hot water had hit her skin, he'd had her against the tiles, his fingers pushing between her legs. She'd tried to beg off, telling him she was too sore, but he'd refused to listen. It had only taken moments for her to come. Chloe had never experienced such all-consuming passion in her life. If she wasn't careful, that man would drive every lucid thought right out of her brain.

Wrapping the towel around her petite frame, she opened the door. Checking the hallway, she didn't see

Logan. Scampering across the cold linoleum floor, she made her way back into the bedroom. On the bed, he had laid out an outfit for her. Her purple babydoll T-shirt with the unicorn graphic on it and a pair of jeans that had a purple sequinned heart on the back pocket. Damn him. It was a cute outfit. Crossing the room, she opened her bureau drawer and began to rummage for a matching bra and panties set.

"What are you doing?"

Chloe jumped. His dark voice startling her.

"I'm looking for underwear." Her voice was soft and apologetic, as if she had just gotten caught with her hand in the cookie jar.

"Do you see any underwear laid out for you?"

Her eyes scanned the bed then returned to him as he lounged against the doorjamb. He had pulled on his pair of jeans. This time he'd added the heavy leather belt. Still, his chest was bare; that magnificent, chiseled chest with all the fascinating tattoos. Seriously! Did the man not own a shirt?

Chloe nervously adjusted the towel between her breasts. She could feel her cheeks start to heat. "No." Her response was barely a whisper.

"No, what?"

Chloe looked at her feet. Her stomach flipped. Between his dominant stance and his authoritative demeanor, she could actually feel her pussy begin to pulse again. *Damn him!*

Licking her lips, she replied, "Please, no."

"My babygirl will only wear a bra and panties when I allow it. Is that clear?"

"Yes, sir."

"Now get dressed. I'm making breakfast."

Chloe hurriedly threw on the jeans and T-shirt. After running her fingers through her damp hair, she made her way to the kitchen where she was greeted by the sweet smell of baking apples.

"Have a seat at the table."

"What are you making?" Her tone was understandably incredulous. Whipping up a quick omelet was one thing, she usually at least had eggs, but anything more adventurous was another.

"After throwing away all the disgusting take-out food containers, I actually found a few apples in your refrigerator. I'm making you a German pancake with apples."

"Seriously? I have the ingredients to make a German pancake?"

"Well, it won't be my best effort," he teased. "You don't have vanilla or lemon juice and I have to use Bisquick instead of flour, but I think it will be edible."

"I have Bisquick?"

Logan laughed as he slid the pancake-filled hot cast iron pan into the oven to finish baking. Taking up his mug, he poured himself a fresh cup of coffee. Then made her a cup of tea with a teaspoon of honey.

Chloe smiled. He had chosen her favorite mug. It was white with gold glitter writing which said 'I got this.' She'd found it in a funny gas station gift store on her way to Michigan from Louisiana. She had taken comfort in the simple phrase, as if the universe had been trying to reassure her everything would be all right.

But it wasn't all right.

Her ex-boyfriend, an escaped convict, was dead by her hand. The man currently standing in the middle of her kitchen playing at being domestic was a dangerous... what? She still didn't fully know. And the fucking cherry on top? She was now on the radar of a violent gang who was searching for a flash drive she still didn't know the whereabouts of.

Yeah. Things were definitely not all right.

Feeling overwhelmed by it all, Chloe focused on something mundane.

"So did the super-secret file you apparently read about me tell you I like tea with honey?"

Logan sat down across from her at the table. The corners of his brilliant blue eyes wrinkled a little bit as he smiled. In the morning light, she could see the spidery, white outline of a scar which cut along his right hairline. Another scar. Another example of the dangerous life this man led.

"I found an old jar of instant coffee in the back of the pantry, but a tin with bags of Lipton and a small container of honey were right out on the counter. It wasn't a big leap to assume you were a tea drinker."

"Oh," she responded lamely as she toyed with the handle of her mug.

"I know you have questions. I'll answer three, if I can."

"Who do you work for?"

"Whoever hires me."

"So did the gang who owns the flash drive hire you?"

"No."

Chloe gave out a frustrated sigh. He was not going to give even a tiny inch. She was anxious to know who hired him, but there was something even more pressing she needed to know.

"You said you wouldn't turn me in to the police for killing Chad. Why not?"

Logan shrugged his shoulders as he took another sip of coffee. "Don't see how it is any of their business."

"But how…."

"That was three. Time to eat."

He rose and pulled the cast iron pan out of the oven. Scooping the contents onto two plates, he returned to the table. Chloe could not help but close her eyes and inhale the creamy scent of melted butter mixed with cinnamon.

Thanking him for the fork he offered, she quickly took a bite and moaned with appreciation.

"Seems like I have a talent for making you moan both in and out of the bedroom," he teased.

"I… I just… don't normally eat this sort of thing for breakfast." Her defensive reply didn't fool him for a moment.

"Once I have you safe and out of this mess, we are going to have a discussion about the junk food and processed crap you think passes for a stable diet."

"I like Chinese food!"

"And you will continue to have it, once in a while, as a treat if you are a good girl. But from now on, you will be eating vegetables and meat that hasn't been battered and fried first," he lectured in that arrogant tone that seemed to always make her stomach twist.

Chloe caught her breath. He made it sound like they were going to be together. Actually, he made it sound as if they were already together. Why on earth would a man like him want to be with someone like her? She'd just murdered someone for heaven's sake! She was not a good person. She was a mess. Hell, she couldn't even feed herself properly! Lowering her eyes, she began to push the remaining pieces of baked apples and bits of pancake around on her plate. She wasn't sure how she felt about all this. Her life had gone from messed up a few years ago to mind-numbingly boring the last two years, to beyond fucked up in the last twenty-four hours. It was a hard swing, and she wasn't sure if Logan was the type to give her time to adjust.

"If all you are going to do is play with the rest of your food, we might as well get back to business."

Chloe felt a nervous flutter in her chest. What did he mean by business? Flashes of him leaning over her as he thrust in deep crossed her mind.

"The flash drive. We still need to find it."

"Oh! Yes, of course! The stupid flash drive," she stammered as she rose to scrape off her plate and put it in the sink. When she turned, she found herself trapped between his arms.

Logan leaned in, his hands resting on the kitchen counter. He searched her eyes.

"My whole life I have broken things. Bad things. Things that deserved to be broken. That's my job. To me, you seem already broken. Existing, not living. A pretty, delicate flower hiding away in the shadows. For once, my job might actually be to fix something. I can see it in your eyes that you don't understand. You don't see yourself the way I do, but you will."

Logan reached up and caressed the corner of her

mouth with the side of his thumb. He brought his thumb to his own mouth. His full lips opened so his tongue could flick out to lick his skin. "You had a bit of sugar on your lip," he explained with a wink.

Chloe melted. Damn him!

* * *

THEY CROSSED the yard to the garage together. Chloe entered the slightly chilled room. Wrapping her arms around her middle, her eyes rested on the discarded .38. It was within arm's length. Now was the moment. She needed to decide. They would probably find the flash drive soon. She stared at the chrome barrel of the gun. Did she trust Logan? Was she going to throw her lot in with him?

Warm hands caressed her exposed arms. Logan spoke over her shoulder. "Are you cold, babygirl? Do you need a jacket?"

She turned her head to see concern in his eyes. Those mercurial blue eyes of his. Giving away nothing one moment, and then showing you his soul the next.

Chloe shook her head, hiding a slight smile. "No. I'm fine." She turned away from the gun and focused on the boxes. She would trust Logan, for now.

Ripping into the second box, Chloe began to rummage through it. When she saw Logan searching the first box, she stopped him. "I already went through that one. Nothing but a lot of old junk."

He ignored her and examined each object one by one.

Shrugging her shoulders, Chloe knelt down and

dumped the contents of the second box out onto the cold cement floor. Honestly, she wasn't even sure why she'd brought this crap with her. Momentary sentimental weakness probably. The second box was filled with costume jewelry, some porcelain knick-knacks and a few scarves. Letting out an excited gasp, Chloe jumped up. In each hand she held one of the two porcelain figurines, a unicorn and a peridot clown.

"I found it!"

Logan looked up.

Chloe raised her arm and threw the clown onto the garage floor, smashing it to pieces. There was nothing inside. "There's still the unicorn. Chad knew I loved unicorns and would probably take this with me," she explained. Without a second thought, she tossed the delicate figurine onto the hard cement floor. It too shattered. Nothing.

Chloe pouted. "I felt for sure that would be it."

Logan gave one of her curls a tug. "It was a good idea, baby. Don't worry. We'll find it. Chad wasn't that smart. I doubt he hid it overly well."

With that, Logan picked up the wretched doll. He stared at the strange white face with the glued-on yarn hair.

"It was Chad's mother's or sister's or something like that. I never liked it. It always looked like the head didn't match the body. Yarn is normally used for hair only on rag dolls. Fucking gave me the creeps."

"Don't curse," ordered Logan absentmindedly as he examined the doll.

"What?"

He looked up, piercing her with a hard look. "I said don't curse. I won't stand for it."

Wait a minute, thought Chloe. That was taking this whole game a little too far. While she hated to admit it, obviously the whole dominant-submissive thing turned her on. She was even okay with how he ordered her about a bit. But to tell her not to fucking curse? What the hell? She wasn't a child. She could fucking curse if she wanted to.

Her eyes widened as Logan slowly put the doll down on the workbench. Oh God! In her fit of pique, she must have said that last part out loud!

Taking slow steps, he circled around the workbench, making his way to the side where she stood. Chloe began to back away at the same time, also circling the bench, doing her best to keep it safely between them.

"What did you just say?" he asked. His brow was lowered and his lips were tight with anger.

Chloe raised her hands protectively in front of her. "I…it's just that…I get the game, but…."

"I've told you before. This is no game." Logan reached for his belt buckle.

"I know the mess with the gang is not a game, but us, the stuff you do, that's a…."

"That's a what, babygirl? Choose your next words carefully," he warned as he pulled the belt free of his jeans.

"I just meant…"

"You just meant what? Because I make you breakfast and let you come, you now think it is okay to break the rules and disrespect me? That is why you are broken, baby. You never respected the rules."

Chloe continued to walk backwards.

"Bend over the workbench," he commanded.

"Here? Outside? Couldn't we just…."

"Bend. Over," he repeated through clenched teeth.

Realizing there was no escape, Chloe bent over and laid her cheek on the smooth wooden surface.

"Now lower your jeans."

Chloe stifled a sob. With shaking fingers, she reached for the brass button which fastened her jeans. She tried appealing to him one more time. "Please. You're right. It's not right to curse."

"Too late. Lower your jeans."

Biting her lip, she pulled on the zipper tab, slowly lowering it. While he looked on, she reached back and pulled the jeans down over her bottom till they rested at the tops of her thighs. Immediately feeling the cold air on her warm skin, Chloe could no longer hold back a sob at her humiliation. The moment she saw him raise his arm, the folded belt in his fist, she covered her face with her hands.

With the first blow of the heavy leather, her knees buckled, only her bent form over the workbench holding her upright. Her entire ass felt like it was covered in bee stings. Then another painful blow. With each successive strike of the belt, her skin became inflamed. And the cold air about her felt like it was making the punishment worse, the heat radiating off her skin a sharp contrast to it.

"It hurts! Please! Stop! I've learned my lesson!" she choked. Her painful sobs made it hard to breathe.

He struck her exposed ass another two times before stopping.

Immediately, Chloe tried to raise her jeans to cover her shame.

"I didn't give you permission to stand up and cover yourself."

With a disgraced sob, she lowered her body onto the hard surface of the workbench once more. The pulsing of her flesh just added to the pain. With each throb, it felt like her skin was getting tighter and hotter as the blood rushed to the surface. Out of the corner of her eye, she watched as he slipped his belt back on. Chloe closed her eyes in relief. Her punishment was over.

She felt his knuckles caress her cheek, wiping away the tears. Still she kept her eyes closed, unable to face him just then.

"What did my baby learn?"

She sniffled. "To obey your rules."

"Good girl. They are for your own good, you know."

"Yes."

"Stay there for a bit longer till I say you may rise."

It was strangely quiet in the garage. Chloe's mind was blank, focused only on the slowly diminishing pain. The whole episode gave her a strange, lightheaded feeling. It was as if the punishment and subsequent crying had been a catharsis. Her mind, which usually raced with any number of random dark, self-deprecating thoughts, quieted. It was as if her mind had shut down, allowing her body to focus on her breathing and still-throbbing bottom. She remained prone across the bench, listening to the rustle of the trees, the odd bird call, the splash of a fish in the water from the nearby lake. How odd that something so emotional, so upsetting, could have such a calming effect!

"You may rise and pull up your jeans."

Chloe slowly rose, feeling hazy and a little off-balance. Gripping the waistband of her jeans, she gingerly pulled them back into place, hissing when the rough denim scraped against her reddened skin. Her cheeks felt sticky and cold where the tears had dried. She rubbed at them with her palms before running a hand through her hair.

Logan approached her, holding his arms open, and she ran into them. He hugged her close. She loved the feel of his thermal shirt against her skin and the musky masculine scent of him. But what she really loved was the feel of his strong arms about her as his hand stroked her hair. "Better?"

She nodded her head.

"Good. Let's get back to the task at hand."

Logan returned to examining the ugly doll. Chloe stood by his side. She watched as he squeezed the body, lifted the skirt, even sniffed at the hair. Finally, he licked the doll's white cheek.

"Ugh! What are you doing? Is that a good idea?"

Logan smiled at her. "You were right. There is something wrong and off about this doll. The head has definitely been replaced. It is compressed cocaine."

"What!"

Chloe stared at the ugly doll in wonder. She reached up to stroke the doll's cheek.

Logan's strong hand enclosed her wrist. "Don't touch it, baby. You see the light dusting on the surface? That is cocaine. You don't want it getting into your system through your fingertips."

Chloe lowered her arm. Of all the stupid crap she had done in her life, heavy drugs hadn't been one of them. She had a healthy respect for and fear of cocaine. Never tried it. Never wanted to, despite Chad trying to force her on several occasions.

"I had no idea Chad was this clever."

"He wasn't. The gang he stole from was experimenting with compressed cocaine in multiple forms. They tried skulls, dolls' heads, dog bones and even mimicking leg and arm casts. From what I remember, they only did a few dolls' heads. The toys looked odd and probably would not have passed the eagle eyes of the customs agents. Chad must have pocketed one of the early prototypes for his own use."

"Not clever, stupid. That sounds more like Chad."

Logan pulled out his bowie knife from inside his biker boot.

Chloe lowered her eyes as she instinctively reached for the metal heart charm. She still hadn't come to terms with the events of the night before, and the knife was a startling reminder.

Using the knife, he carefully cut into the thick stuffing of the doll's body. Tearing open the flaps, there, tucked deep inside, was the shiny glint of black plastic. The flash drive.

"You found it!" she exclaimed.

"We found it."

"My computer is upstairs in my workshop. Should we plug it in and see if it has the bank accounts?"

"No. This is it. There may be some kind of tracing software or virus protecting it. Best to just give it to my client and let them deal with the consequences," responded Logan as he dropped the flash drive into his jeans pocket as if it were a tin of mints and not the key to fifteen million dollars.

Chloe was stunned. He really didn't give a damn about the money. He had told her that when they'd first met, but she hadn't believed him, hadn't trusted his response.

"You really don't care? This really is just a job to you."

"It was just a job. It became something more, because of you, not because of this blood money. Trust me, baby. You don't want the karma associated with shit like this. It brings bad men like me into your life." He tugged affectionately on one of her curls.

Chloe giggled despite the seriousness of the situation. Pointing to him, she teased, "You said a bad word."

She laughed as he chased her back into the cabin.

CHAPTER 10

"Are you going to leave now that you have the drive?"

He looked down at Chloe. Her cheeks were pink. Her lips bright red and swollen. Disheveled locks of hair framed her face. They both lay sprawled amidst the rumpled covers and sheets of the bed.

"*We* are leaving tonight as soon as it gets dark."

"I thought once you had the drive…."

"You're not out of danger yet, babygirl. That gang figured out Chad double-crossed them the moment he cleared those prison grounds. They are probably already on their way up here. We need to clear out. I'll get you to safety then make the exchange with my client. As soon as the gang learns you no longer have the drive, they will leave you alone."

"Won't they still try to come after me…for revenge or something? That is what they do in the movies."

He chuckled as he kissed the top of her head. "Unlikely. Killing a young white woman would be bad for business and bring too much attention. Not that they wouldn't hesitate to do so if they thought you were still in possession of the drive," he qualified.

"How do we let them know? It's not like I can email them."

"Let's just say I have a few connections. I'll get the word to them in no uncertain terms."

"Won't they go after your client next?"

Logan smiled. "That's my client's problem."

To lighten the mood, he said, "Besides, we have to leave or we will starve. There is literally no more food in this cabin."

She gave him a playful swat on the arm, her hand resting on his queen of hearts tattoo.

* * *

"Pack only what you need."

"But I *need* all my tools and supplies," she complained, as she started stacking tools and jewelry molds on the workbench in her studio above the garage.

Logan reached out to still her hands.

Cupping her by the shoulders, he said, "Baby, we came up here because you said you needed something from the safe, not to pack up your whole damn life. I am trying to save you from a psychotic gang, you know."

Her lower lip protruded in an adorable pout.

"I am packing up the safe. There are lots of precious stones and metals in there. Not to mention those stupid diamonds. I don't see why I couldn't also take a few tools and supplies. I have an order to fill. I still have to make a living."

Logan threw up his hands in defeat. Now was not the time to tell Chloe her life had changed the moment that piece of shit ex-boyfriend of hers implicated her in a theft from a powerful Columbian gang. The likelihood of her returning to her jewelry business was slim at best. He would save that revelation for later, when he had her safe.

He placed a single large box in the center of the room. "You may fill this box... *and only this box*... with anything you want from here."

Chloe gave him a peck on the cheek. "You come off as all mean and dangerous, but you can be a real softie, you know?"

He gave her a swat on the ass as he playfully growled at her.

"I will be back."

"Where are you going?" There was a hint of anxiety in her voice. Logan smiled. He liked that she had gotten so used to his presence that it concerned her when he left. It felt good to have someone give a damn about him. It had been too long.

"I need to head into the woods and grab the coordinates for Chad's grave. I wasn't able to do it with any accuracy last night in the dark and the rain."

The mention of Chad's body sobered the moment.

Chloe shuffled and rearranged the metal molds on her workbench. "Do you think I am an evil person? Not for killing him; I truly believe it was in my own self-defense. There is not a doubt in my mind he would have killed me first. But for not caring more?"

Logan wrapped his arms around her middle and pulled her close. Back to front. He nuzzled her neck. "You care. Trust me, baby. You are not so far gone to the dark side yet that you could kill without emotion or guilt. The emotional reaction will come later, once the danger has passed and you have time to really think on it. But don't worry, I'll be there. I'll get you through it."

"I supposed you've killed countless men?" she asked hesitantly as she stroked his hand which rested protectively over her middle.

"Yes, but they were all bad," he said off-handedly. Turning her around, he gave her a kiss on the forehead and headed down the stairs.

* * *

Chloe's scream pierced the silence of the woods.

Logan bolted, racing under branches and over fallen logs.

Finally, the cabin came into view.

Another scream.

Fuck!

He vaulted over the wooden fence marking the edge of her uncle's property. Leaning his back against the side of the cabin, he slowed his breathing and focused. He wouldn't be any good to Chloe if he ran into the situation half-cocked.

Sliding along the wall, he could hear voices as he neared the front clearing. There were more than one, possibly three men. Hispanic accents.

"Shut the dumb bitch up. You want to alert that asshole?"

"Did you see the size of that fucker?"

"What, you scared, Julio?"

"Fuck you. I'm not scared of anyone. I'm just saying he's a big fucking dude."

"That big fucking dude is going to kill you for touching me."

The last was from his girl. Feisty and full of fire as always. Damn, he loved the spitfire in her. He would even forgive her cursing, this time.

"Shut up, *puta*."

There was the sickening sound of skin-on-skin contact.

He had heard enough. Logan strolled into view.

All conversation stopped. All eyes were on him.

One man stepped forward, puffing his chest in a fool's attempt to look important and authoritative. It didn't work.

"Stop where you are. We are US Marshals taking this woman into custody for harboring a fugitive." The man's tone was formal and no-nonsense. The perfect mimic of a government official…from a Hollywood movie.

Logan wasn't buying it. He assessed the scene.

The three men were also dressed rather comically as S.W.A.T. commandos, apparently falling for the complete Hollywood package of what US Marshals wear. Even the badges on their chests were wrong. They each had a four-point star pinned to their shirts, not the traditional six-point star of the Marshal service.

The final tell? Their hardware. They were each

carrying FN Five-seveN pistols, not the standard government-issued Glock. The gun was nicknamed the *cop-killer* because its ammunition could puncture bulletproof vests and even light armored cars. It was a favorite among the Mexican cartels.

A Mexican cartel? *Jesus Christ.* This whole thing was becoming a real clusterfuck.

He couldn't wait to get back in front of his client. He would definitely have a few choice words regarding the briefing he'd received about this job. Well, at least he would try to contain his remarks to just words.

It looked like the message had finally gotten out that the Columbians had a rogue member. Now the Mexicans had arrived to claim Chloe and the flash drive. It didn't make sense why the Mexicans were getting involved in this mess; the Colombians were their cocaine suppliers. Still, Logan wouldn't put it past some upstart Mexican cartel to try to make a name for themselves by retrieving the flash drive just to fuck with the Colombians.

So basically, the Mexicans and the Columbians were about to get into a petty pissing match over a measly fifteen million, and his Chloe was caught in the middle. If that fucking piece of shit Chad hadn't already been dead he would kill him himself, thought Logan, and not for the first time.

Holding his hands high in the air, Logan slowly approached the armed men.

Chloe's arms were pulled back behind her by one of the men. The other two eyed him anxiously, guns drawn.

Heedless of their threat, he boldly walked straight up to Chloe. Reaching out, he stroked her cheek, lightly touching a small bit of blood from a cut on her cheekbone.

His clever girl deliberately shifted her eyes to a man with bleached hair before looking back at him. That was the man who'd hit her. Logan couldn't wait to break both his arms.

"Back away from the prisoner," said the first man, the one with KILL tattooed across his right knuckles.

"Do you know who I am?" asked Logan in a conversational tone as his narrowed gaze fell on each man individually.

The third man, his mouth filled with gold-capped teeth, answered, dropping the pretense of their disguise. "Yeah. We know. Our boss doesn't want any trouble. We're just here to take the girl and the drive. This doesn't involve you anymore."

Logan chuckled as he slowly cracked his knuckles, one by one. "Oh, this won't be any trouble at all. I'm going to kill each one of you and then continue on with the job."

The three men exchanged worried glances.

Logan had a fierce reputation with both sides, the legal and the not-so-legal. He was certain that if fifteen million dollars hadn't been at stake, this particular gang would not have knowingly waded into his territory. Whatever Mexican gang or cartel this was, they had balls, he would give them that.

"In case you can't count, bro, there's three of us and only one of you, and I don't see any gun," said the bleached blond as he pointed his Five-seveN at Logan.

Logan nodded his agreement. "Funny thing about guns. It gives assholes a false sense of their own abilities."

Logan's hand struck out, grabbing the closest man's gun as he planted his right foot to the side and pulled with all his weight. The gang member with the tattooed knuckles lurched forward. As he tripped over Logan's foot and tumbled to the ground, Logan maintained his grip on the gun. Holding the man's arm outstretched, he stepped on the elbow joint, breaking it. The man screamed in agony. Logan kicked him in the jaw, his heavy biker boot striking the surprisingly fragile bone and breaking it as well, knocking the man unconscious.

Picking up a large rock near the edge of the driveway, Logan turned to bleach blond. "Your turn," he said ominously. His eyes narrowed their focus on the gang member who'd hit Chloe. As the man raised his gun, Logan hefted the large rock and threw it at his head, striking him in the temple. The man staggered back, dropping his gun. Logan grabbed one of the man's wrists and, twisting both their hands clockwise, broke it. As bleach blond reached for his broken wrist, Logan grabbed the man's arm and twisted it painfully behind his back until he heard the bone snap. The man fell to his knees in agony.

Logan retrieved the man's gun and turned it on him. "Your co-workers here? I'll let live. You? You touched my woman."

"Please," the man begged as his broken arms hung limply.

Without pause, ignoring his pathetic pleas, Logan pulled the trigger...just to the right of the kneeling man, into the dirt.

A dark stain spread across the front of the man's pants

a moment before he collapsed in a heap. Fainting from fear or pain, probably both. Logan smirked. That should send enough of a message.

He turned in time to see Chloe attacking her assailant. The man had her around the throat. First, she stepped on his foot. When he released his grip, she bent in half. Swiveling her torso, she viciously elbowed the man in his stomach. The moment he was distracted from the pain, she turned in his arms. Resting her hands on the man's shoulders for leverage, she drew up her knee and nailed him square in the groin. The man howled in pain as he doubled over, clutching his middle, but Logan's feisty little fighter wasn't done with the Mexican gang member yet. Grabbing the bent-over man by the hair on the back of his head, she brought her knee up a second time, breaking his nose. The man fell to the ground, beaten.

"Damn, babygirl. You unmanned him," said Logan with pride.

Chloe limped toward Logan. Rubbing her lower leg, she complained, "Before Bleached Gangland Barbie over there slapped my face, that one kicked me in the shin. What kind of schoolyard bullshit is that? You know how much it hurts to be kicked in the shin?"

Logan wrapped his hand around the back of her neck and pulled her in for a quick kiss. "Don't ever change, my dark angel."

Chloe blushed from the endearment.

Recovering, she grumbled as she rubbed her leg. "This is totally going to bruise."

"I'll kiss your boo-boo and make it better later, for

now I have to get these assholes tied up. Are your bags packed?"

She nodded.

Logan raised an eyebrow. "How many bags? You didn't fill more than that box with your work tools did you?"

Chloe shook her head. "Just the box and my pink gym bag."

"Good girl." Logan tossed her his keys. "Load them up in my truck while I clean up this mess."

"Are you...are you going to kill them?" she asked hesitantly.

"They are very bad men, baby," he reasoned.

Chloe nodded her head .

"But no, they're worth more as leverage."

"Leverage?"

"You'll see."

One by one Logan dragged the limp bodies into a small shed across from the garage. From the look of it, it had been used for butchering when her late uncle had hunted on this property.

Perfect, thought Logan.

Securing the men's wrists with rope, he hung each of them from sturdy metal hooks which dangled from the ceiling. Hooks usually used to bleed the hunter's kill. He then secured their ankles. He didn't bother to gag them. The cabin was so remote no one would hear their cries for help, but that wouldn't stop them from screaming themselves hoarse trying.

Since the earliest Logan would send someone to retrieve them was late tomorrow, they would probably all have permanent nerve damage from dangling so long by their arms. He doubted any of the three gang members would be able to hold a gun or threaten another unarmed woman again.

A fitting punishment.

That is, if their own gang let them live after this bungled job.

An even more fitting punishment, thought Logan.

He left the dark, dank shed. Closing the double doors, he found a large, sturdy stick and drove it through the metal handles, securing the door as an extra precaution.

They would stay put until Logan had a chance to use them against both his client and the Columbians.

Chloe was already waiting for him in his 4-Runner. He hopped in on the driver's side. He gave her hand a playful slap when she reached for the radio.

"There is one major rule in my truck. Only I touch the radio," he teased.

"Please don't tell me you like..." The rest of her sentence was a groan as the opening strains of some country song belted over the airwaves.

"Buckle your seat belt, little lady. We have a long ride."

* * *

THEY RODE in silence for at least five hours, both alone in their own thoughts. Hours spent listening to country songs with lyrics about a wholesome America filled with love, horses and picket fences. About an existence neither of them had ever known.

When he turned onto the Skyway, Chloe turned to

him in confusion. "Are we going to Chicago? I would have thought...well..."

Logan laughed. "What? You figured I was taking you to some safe house? Maybe a small farm in the middle of Kentucky?"

Chloe twisted the cord of the hoodie she had folded on her lap around her finger. "Well, yes!"

Logan ran his knuckles down her cheek before grasping one silken brown curl and giving it a playful tug. "No, baby. That's only in the movies. The safest place to hide is in plain sight in the middle of a crowd. Besides, my client is in Chicago."

She gave him a sideways glance.

"Are you going to tell me who it is?"

"I think it's best you don't know. The less you know about this mess, the safer you will be in the long run."

They both slipped back into a pensive silence.

An hour later, the distinctive outline of the Chicago skyline came into view. They rolled down Lakeshore Drive. Lake Michigan appeared dark and foreboding with only the occasional whitecap in the fading light. Logan's black 4-Runner pulled up to the valet at the Drake Hotel.

"The Drake?" That amused Chloe. "Well, I guess there goes another assumption."

Logan spared her a quick glance. "I can't stand two-bit motels. Crappy beds and no room service."

Chloe laughed as she got out of the truck.

"Leave it out front," instructed Logan to the valet as he handed him a twenty.

The valet nodded as he quickly pocketed the hefty tip. "Yes, sir."

Logan waved away the porter who tried to unload their bags. "I got them."

As they spun through the revolving door and walked up the royal blue carpeted stairs, Logan saw a look of wonder cross her face as the ornate lobby came into view.

Chloe blushed when she noticed his regard.

"Sorry. I've never really stayed in a place so luxurious. I mean I've stayed at nice hotels, just not the kind that have flower arrangements the size of small cars and porters dressed like organ monkeys," she giggled.

Logan placed a protective hand on her lower back as he guided her to the reception desk.

"We'll take a suite for the night."

"Yes, sir. Credit card and ID please."

Logan fished the cards out of his wallet. Trying to keep Chloe from reading the names, he placed them face down on the counter.

After several minutes of tapping at keys, the front desk manager handed back his cards. "I have you booked in a suite on our third floor. Here are your two key cards. I hope you enjoy your stay, Mr.—"

Logan cut the woman off. "Thank you. We will."

Ignoring Chloe's questioning look, he motioned to the elevators.

When they arrived at the room, he leaned over her shoulder, slid the key card into the lock and opened the door. Shouldering her pink gym bag and his black duffel, Logan preceded her inside the room, doing a quick sweep of the parlor area, bedroom and bathroom.

"You don't think a gang member is lurking behind the shower curtain do you?"

"Force of habit," Logan said as he dropped the bags to the floor.

The hotel room fell silent. Logan stood across from Chloe, taking in the sight of her. It was the first time he had been able to breathe easily since he'd heard her scream from across the woods earlier that afternoon.

He took a step toward her a moment before she ran into his arms. Spearing his fingers into her dark tresses, Logan angled her head back. Staring down into her expressive, stormy gray eyes, he said, "Don't ever scare me like that again."

Tears spiked her eyelashes. "I'll try not to."

His mouth took possession of hers. Forcing his tongue past her lips, he tasted deeply. His tongue swirled and teased her own. Lightly rubbing his teeth against her plump lower lip, he rasped against her mouth, "I'm going to fuck you till you forget everything from today but my touch."

Chloe moaned as he palmed her breast through the thin fabric of her babydoll T-shirt. Rubbing his thumb over the erect nipple, Logan walked forward, thrusting her against the wall. Placing both hands high above her head, he ground his hips against her own. He groaned from the pressure as his hard cock was squeezed between their bodies. He took her mouth again.

Biting. Tasting.

Lowering his arms, he ran his hands over her ribcage, pushing up her T-shirt. The moment her breasts were exposed, he leaned down to suck one pink nipple into his mouth, nipping it with his teeth while he palmed the other. Inhaling deeply, he took in the warm vanilla scent of her skin. With a growl, he ripped the T-shirt over her head. Opening his mouth, Logan sucked on the delicate skin of her neck.

Biting. Tasting.

Her hands clutched at his hair, pulling hard. The kiss of pain just spurred him on.

Tearing at her jeans, he slipped the brass button through its hole and lowered the zipper. Driving his right hand between her legs, he palmed her pussy while his left hand pushed on the fabric, lowering the jeans to her ankles. Pushing one, then two fingers into her wet heat, he thrust them in and out while his thumb caressed her clit.

"Oh God! Oh God!" Her open mouth skated along his flesh, kissing the bloodred petals of his tattoo.

Logan reached under her knees and lifted her high, bracing her against the wall with the pressure from his hips. As she wrapped her legs around his middle, he reached between them under her right leg, and lowered the zipper of his jeans. His cock sprang free, hard and wanting. Grabbing onto her thighs, he shifted his hips till the head of his cock was at her tight entrance, teasing her.

"Who's in charge?" he growled.

"You are... oh God! You are!"

Chloe screamed as he speared her with his cock. Pressing her against the hard surface of the wall, he pummeled into her welcoming cunt, feeling her tight muscles clench and grasp at his shaft. He licked at a small drop of sweat glistening between her breasts. He felt as if he were an animal crazed with lust. The need to possess and mark her was strong. Without thought,

Logan bit down on her shoulder. Her cry of pain sent him into a frenzy. He licked at the faint red crescent marks.

"Do it again. Make it hurt," she begged.

Logan opened his mouth over the top of her breast. Pulling her soft flesh between his lips, sucking, he bit down again.

Marking her again.

Throwing his head back with a roar, he thrust harder. Pounding into her small frame. Dominating her with brute strength.

"Say it," he ground out through clenched teeth as he felt his balls tighten. His stomach contracted with need. "Say it."

"Fuck me," she breathed against his neck.

With a guttural shout, he released deep inside her.

Marking her with his seed.

The cries of her release mixed with his heavy breathing. Clasping his arms about her, he turned. Keeping his cock buried inside her cunt, he collapsed on the bed, rolling with her in his arms. Pinning her beneath him, he brushed back her hair. Taking in her swollen lips and flushed cheeks, he felt a surge of primal possession.

She was his and he'd be damned if he let anyone harm her again.

* * *

An hour later, Logan was dressed in a fresh shirt and pair of jeans. He had tucked Chloe into bed. Giving her a kiss on the forehead, he said, "I will be a few hours. Do not leave this room. You can order room service but no junk food."

Chloe pouted. "What's the fun in ordering hotel room service if you can't order junk food?"

"I mean it young lady. Something healthy."

She gave him a cheeky grin. "Is a cheeseburger healthy?"

Flicking the tip of her nose, he said, "Order it and you will find out my answer when I get back."

His grasping the buckle of his belt as he responded told Chloe all she needed to know about what his answer would be.

Opening the door, Logan tossed over his shoulder, "And no scary movies. I expect to see a rom-com on the hotel invoice."

Chloe snuggled further into the blankets with a smile. He waited till he saw her lift the remote and start to search under romantic comedies before closing the door.

CHAPTER 11

Chloe counted to ten before throwing the covers off. Walking over to the door, she looked out the peephole. The hotel hallway was empty. Grabbing her jeans off the floor, she stepped into them as she reached for her T-shirt. She didn't know how long Logan would be, but she needed to be far away before he got back.

Tears filled her eyes at the thought of leaving him. She knew it was purely about leaving him and not the thought of being on her own. She had already lived through escaping one dangerous situation with the possibility of a pissed off gang on her heels. Granted, this time was worse and the stakes way higher, but still. The tears were for Logan.

The fact that she had found herself in this position before was why she was leaving.

You might not be able to escape your past, but you could make damn sure you didn't repeat it.

She had already been to this rodeo. Fallen for the dangerous guy, the bad boy. Loving the excitement.

Relishing in how her life wasn't just some ordinary nine-to-five drudge. The problem was it would end badly. She couldn't imagine a scenario where it wouldn't. She thought back to all those country songs. Fuck the white picket fence. It wasn't in the cards for her.

Chloe swiped at tears as she pulled on her sneakers. Damn him. Damn him for making her care. Damn him for making her actually feel something again. Damn him for chasing away the numbness. Damn him for making her feel protected and actually cared for. It was all a lie anyway. She'd seen a glimpse of his ID when he'd put it back in his wallet. He'd tried to keep it from her, but she'd seen it. The first name did not begin with an "L". It looked more like "Jo." John? Joseph? Goddammit. Not only had she never even gotten his last name from him, now it looked like she didn't even know his first!

How?

How the fuck had she gotten herself into this kind of mess again? First Chad and now Logan.

Chloe's erratic thoughts paused. Even in her hurt and anger, she knew she was being unfair. Logan was nothing like Chad. Chad had been a thug, a corrupt cop…a bully. Sure, Logan could be brutal and even downright mean at times, but she'd learned it had actually been to protect her. His methods, while unorthodox, were apparently just what she needed. Finally, because of him, she could let go of the guilt she'd felt about that night in Louisiana. Instead of constantly beating herself up, trying to turn herself into something she wasn't, she could now learn to accept all her twisty, messed up sides, the dark and light ones. Because of him.

She wasn't perfect, and the crazy thing was, she honestly believed that was what Logan liked about her. Maybe even loved. Her beautiful fucked up imperfections.

Hell, the man had actually covered up a murder for her. And at this moment was meeting with his client to arrange it so she was never bothered by anyone again.

So why was she running?

Because she had already been to this rodeo, that was why.

It was a fun, dramatic, heart-pounding thrill ride, but eventually you got bucked off and found yourself face-down in the dirt.

No, Logan wasn't like Chad. He was far more dangerous.

She'd never thought of Chad as anything more than a boyfriend. She'd always known eventually she would wise up and ditch his ass. Probably when the fun stopped, and it definitely had stopped that night. She couldn't imagine the same scenario with Logan. Strange, but she didn't even think of him in boyfriend terms. That term was too lighthearted, too commonplace, too vanilla. He was something deeper, more intense, more raw, than simply a boyfriend.

A man who protected and disciplined. A man who cared for her, and not in that superficial way, but in every way, from whether she was safe to whether she ate her vegetables and dressed warmly. A man who was doing everything possible to shield her from the harsh realities of the world as well as the consequences of her own mistakes, past and present. A man who had filled her life with passion as well as real affection.

Problem was he had done too good of a job. She now recognized she'd been hiding from herself, from life, up at that cabin. It was time to get back to the living, to actually create a real life for herself. It didn't have to be a boring nine-to-five drudge, but it also wasn't going to be following around some mercenary on dangerous jobs. She figured that was what Logan had to be. A hired killer. The kind of person you turned to when you didn't want to get the law involved. He got paid to, how did he put it? Clean up messes.

Well, she was a mess. He'd cleaned her up. His job was over.

Besides, it wasn't like he was really serious about wanting her to stay by his side. He had bad boy loner written all over him. As soon as the excitement of this job was over, he would probably split anyway. Back to some femme fatale named Nikita or Sasha.

Chloe could hear Logan's amused voice in her head, teasingly reminding her once again that this wasn't a Hollywood movie, and real men didn't date women named Nikita. Well, he would probably say that, after he finished punishing her for cursing so much...even in her thoughts.

Her stomach twisted. Was she doing the right thing? Should she stay and at least talk to him about how she was feeling?

No. It would only make their parting more difficult, more awkward. It would probably even ruin her memories of him. She risked him telling her that the whole attraction thing was a sham, a game to get her cooperation.

Deep down, she felt that was wrong. It had been real. Well, maybe it had been or maybe it hadn't.

She had made mistakes before. Her past was riddled with them. What was one more?

Chloe grabbed her bag and headed for the door. Thinking better of it, she turned back. Throwing her bag on the bed, she rummaged through the desk till she found a hotel pad and pen. After a few failed attempts to get the pen to work, she finally scratched out a quick, completely insufficient, note. Chloe then dug through her gym bag till she found the one thing which she hoped would help him understand. She left it on top of the note.

How odd. The most intense experience of her life and it ended with an "I'm sorry" note scratched out on a hotel notepad.

It seemed a mistake to do it this way, but then that was what she was good at, mistakes.

Chloe picked up her bag and left.

CHAPTER 12

Logan pulled into the small parking lot of the Golden Nugget on the north side of Chicago. Meeting at a diner at ten o'clock at night was a little cloak and dagger for his taste, but that was how this particular client liked it. Pulling open the glass door, he surveyed the dining room. At this hour, the booths were filled with loud teenagers, cops grabbing a bite before their graveyard shift and a few blue-collars, which, of course, meant his client stuck out like a sore thumb. Logan slid into the third booth on the right. Across from him were two men, both with cheap haircuts and cheaper suits.

"Jesus Christ, Bob, why don't you just duct tape your badge to your forehead? It would be less subtle," Logan laughed as he signaled the server for a cup a coffee.

"Keep your voice down. We don't want the world to know what we are doing here," groused Bob's partner.

"Relax, Tom. You could fire off your weapon in here, and the only thing any of these people would give two shits about is if the scene was going to delay their pancakes."

The server snickered at his remark as she poured his coffee.

Giving him an appreciative look, she asked, "Can I get you anything?"

"Just the coffee, thanks," responded Logan, giving the buxom blonde only the barest of glances.

He had a girl now. A sweet little broken doll. He was going to get them both away from all this dark shit and make a real life with her. Logan smiled at the thought.

"So you have the drive?" asked Bob anxiously.

Logan's only response was a nod.

"Well, let's see it."

Tom was already opening up his laptop to check out the veracity of the flash drive.

"There are a few things we need to renegotiate first," said Logan as he leaned back in his seat, raising an arm over the back.

"The F.B.I doesn't renegotiate. Your fee is your fee. It was already hell getting that through all the red tape. I'm not going back to ask for more, Logan," warned Bob.

"First, cut the bullshit. You're not F.B.I., you're C.I.A."

Bob and Tom exchanged glances.

"And just how do you suppose that?"

Logan took a leisurely sip of his coffee, enjoying making them wait. "It's your guns. You can change your outfit and even flash a costume badge, but people will rarely carry a different weapon from their own. The F.B.I.'s current standard issue is a Glock 22 or 23. You both are carrying Beretta 92s, the preferred firearm of

C.I.A. agents. You think I would take a job and not make damn fucking sure I knew who I was working with?"

Bob rubbed his jaw and gave Logan a resigned look. "You're good. Okay, on the level. We can't work domestic shit. You know that. We're helping clean up the mess from that A.T.F. gunwalking scandal. Off the record of course. Orders come straight from the Oval. He wants it handled. Stretching the rules since it involves Mexico."

Logan nodded his head. Operation Fast and Furious. The A.T.F. looked the other way while gun dealers sold to illegal buyers in Mexico. The hope was they could trace the guns back to the Mexican cartels and eventually cut off their firepower supply. It had failed. Spectacularly. The A.T.F. lost track of more than half of the guns sold. In fact, that was how the cartels had actually gotten their hands on the military-issued-only FN Five-seveNs. The guns lost had been used in crimes on both sides of the border. It was a fucking mess and a PR nightmare that hadn't gone away even years later. Every time the scandal fizzled, someone died from a gun traced back to Fast and Furious and the whole shitstorm got kicked up again.

"So how does the flash drive play in?"

"When we heard about the missing flash drive, we figured if we could get our hands on it first, we could use it to leverage the Columbians. We return the flash drive in exchange for their help in tracking some of the guns through their end clients, the Mexican cartels. At this point, we just want those particular guns destroyed. We don't care about anything else. We think they'll play ball. They want this flash drive bullshit over as much as we want the Fast and Furious guns, and they have leverage over the cartels we don't have...they control the cocaine supply. It's a win-win."

"And, of course, you're old friends with the Columbians," taunted Logan, referring to the theory the C.I.A. had been heavily involved in the early cocaine trade in Los Angeles in the 80s.

"That has never been proven," objected Tom. Bob put a restraining hand on his arm.

"It makes for a nice lead-in. The Mexicans might be onto what you are trying to do. They sent a crew after the drive," offered Logan.

"What happened?"

"What do you think happened?" shot back Logan. "You'll find them tied up at Chloe's cabin. Here are the coordinates." Logan handed him a small piece of paper. "This also has the coordinates to a shallow grave deep in the woods."

"Do I want to know?" asked Bob.

Logan shrugged. "Let's just say you can also tell the Columbians you took care of their little HR problem for them."

Bob nodded his approval. "Actually, that could help with our negotiations with them. So, what did you want to renegotiate?"

"I want Chloe's name scrubbed from this whole mess." Logan reached back and pulled out a worn file, folded in half, from the back pocket of his jeans. He tossed the red folder on the table. "In there you will find every instance where her name intersects with Chad's and the Columbians. Take care of it, and make sure the Columbians understand she is no longer a part of this."

Bob raised his eyebrows. "That's all. You don't want more money?"

"Nothing I ever do is about the money. This is worth far more to me. See that it gets done."

Bob nodded as he tucked the folder into his laptop bag. Logan was confident it would be. No one double-crossed a man of his reputation.

"Good." He kicked back the last of his coffee. "Pleasure doing business with you," Logan said with a smile as he rose to take his leave.

"Wait. The burner number you gave us. It doesn't work anymore. The contact we used to find you also said he can't get a hold of you either. How do we reach you if we need you for another job?"

"You don't. I'm retiring," said Logan.

He turned and left the diner, anxious to get back to his babygirl.

The whole fucking mess had been cleaned up. His job was over.

It was time to start thinking about a future with Chloe.

* * *

He returned to the room to find her gone.

Walking over to the desk, he picked up the purple Crown Royal bag and upended the contents into his palm. It looked to be over a 100 large cut diamonds. He shifted his hand and watched how they glittered in the soft lamplight. Low-grade cloudiness aside, they were still diamonds.

He picked up the note beside them. The words might

have explained that she couldn't bear to repeat her past mistakes by falling in love with a dangerous man, and how the diamonds represented how close she had come to succumbing to that dark life before, but he saw the true meaning behind the note.

His bedeviled angel had just grown wings.

Logan picked up the phone with his free hand and instructed the front desk to have the valet bring around his truck. He was checking out.

Looked like he wasn't retiring after all, he thought as he poured the diamonds back into the bag. He had one more job to complete.

And his new client had just paid him in advance.

CHAPTER 13

Montreal, Canada
One month later

"Celui-là est mon préféré!"

Chloe looked up at her friend Marianne. "All of them are your favorites," she laughed.

Chloe went back to arranging her jewelry inside the display case. She rented out the case at a cute jewelry boutique inside the Marche Bonsecours. It was a nice arrangement. The historic market was located on St. Paul Street in the heart of the tourist district of Montreal. On her own, she would never have been able to afford a shop in such a prime location, but she could afford to rent a display case inside of one and, who knew? Perhaps one day she would have her own little shop. It would be just what she needed. A business to focus all her energies on. A business to fill the void.

Giving herself a mental shake, Chloe tried to force

away thoughts of *him*. It had been an entire month, and not one day, or truth be told, not one hour, had gone by without her thinking of Logan. The way he used to brush his knuckles down her cheek or teasingly pull on one of her curls. How sexy he'd looked dressed in only jeans with his bare, tattoo-covered chest on display as he'd moved about the cabin's small kitchen making her that apple pancake. It was pathetic. Even the scent of coffee brought back memories of his large, tanned hands cupping a mug as he leaned nonchalantly against the doorjamb.

Then, of course, thoughts of his hands brought back thoughts of him bathing her in the shower, of him holding her down as he fucked her, of the feel of his hand as he disciplined her. She even missed his spankings. The feel of his leather belt after she had done something bad. The other day she had said the word fuck out loud, and tears had pricked her eyes when she realized no one cared if she used bad language. It was such a silly little thing, but still. It hurt to think no one cared.

She missed him.

For a few weeks, every time she heard a knock on a door, which was usually for the apartment next door and never for her, she thought it might be him. She would catch a glimpse of a tall man in a crowd, and her heart would skip for just the barest of moments till she realized it was not him. Even the ring of the little shop bell would always cause her stomach to flutter.

Now that a month had passed, she had to come to terms with the fact that he was not coming after her. She realized now that that was one of the reasons why she'd run. True, she'd needed to prove to herself that she could create a life without anyone's help, that she was capable of not making a hot mess of everything. Still, there was a small part of her that had hoped he would follow. That he would find her like he had done before. That he would prove that she hadn't been just a job. That she could see pride in his face when he saw her pretty jewelry case.

"*Non! Non! Dites-le en français,*" admonished Marianne, bringing Chloe back to the present.

Chloe groaned. "*Non*! When I asked you to teach me French, it was because I thought everyone spoke only French here, and I would be lost. They don't! Everyone speaks English too. I get along just fine."

"Tsk. Tsk. Tsk. You are a very stubborn girl," said Marianne as she wagged her finger at Chloe. "You need to learn your French if you are truly going to become a Montrealer."

"I will. I will," placated Chloe.

"How about a drink after work? There is someone I would like you to meet, yes?"

Marianne had tried to fix her up with countless friends, friends of friends, customers, even one man she'd met in a shop the other day. Chloe always said no. There was only truly one man for her, and she'd ruined it.

Chloe shook her head. "No thank you. I think I will just head home early tonight." Chloe locked her display and began to gather her things.

"Oh! How silly of me! I almost forgot. There was a handsome man in here while you were on the lower level chatting with the owner of the bookshop. He admired your jewelry. I tried to sell him something, but he said he wanted to meet the artist of such beautiful pieces and buy from her directly. He will be back tomorrow," said Marianne.

Chloe nodded and thanked her before leaving. A week ago, maybe even a few days ago, a message like would have had her wondering, but not now.

* * *

CHLOE RUBBED her neck as she looked forlornly at the contents of her fridge. Indian food was Montreal's counterpart to American Chinese take-out. She stared at the containers of samosas, chicken tandoori and shrimp vindaloo. She turned her nose up at it all. Again, as frequent as her own heartbeat, a thought of Logan came into her mind, unbidden. She could hear his voice chastising her for eating junk food and ordering her to eat a vegetable. Closing the fridge, she went into the bedroom to change out of her skirt and blouse and into a pair of jeans and T-shirt. Perhaps doing a little gardening would cheer her up. She rented a little apartment that was one of four in a small building on a quiet cul-de-sac. Her favorite part was the cute common garden in the backyard that all the renters worked in. It couldn't replace the beautiful lake and surrounding woods of her uncle's cabin, but it was a small piece of nature inside the city, and it was one of her few comforts.

Chloe was kneeling in the dirt when she heard a car pull up in the cul-de-sac. In Montreal, it was very popular to bike or walk. Cars were not as common as in America, so the sound of one in the gathering dusk struck her as odd. Rising, she brushed the dirt from her knees and made her way into her apartment. As she was crossing through the kitchen, there was a knock…on her door this time. It was a deep, strong knock. The kind that rattled the door on its hinges.

She took a step back, gripping the metal heart charm around her neck.

"Chloe. Open the door."

She stared at the door with wide eyes. He had found her. Oh God. He had found her. She suddenly couldn't breathe. Her heart started to race. Chloe stood there frozen.

There was a long, excruciating pause.

Then.

"I know you are in there. I need you to open the door, babygirl."

She had missed the dark command of his voice.

"Baby, I'm losing my patience. Trust me. You don't want that."

Snapping out of her shock, Chloe leaned over and turned the lock before taking a fidgety step back again.

She watched as the doorknob slowly turned.

The old, wooden door swung open.

Logan.

Dressed in faded jeans and a fitted black T-shirt, she could see hints of his tattoos peeking out from the edges of his collar and sleeves. Rough stubble covered his jaw, and it looked like he hadn't cut his hair in the month they'd been apart. Slightly longer, it fell in soft waves over his forehead and a little over his ears, but it was the dark focused look in his blue eyes that arrested her.

"I'm home, babygirl," he growled before kicking the

door shut with his heavy motorcycle boot and dropping his black duffel on the floor.

Chloe backed up a step as she raised her hands protectively before her.

"I can explain!"

"Really? You can explain why you would run away from my protection? Why you would leave nothing but this note!"

Reaching into his back pocket, he pulled out a well-worn, folded piece of paper.

Chloe's heart lurched. He had kept her note.

"I needed to be on my own. To actually experience a real life, not one filled with chaos and blood or isolation and boredom, but just a normal life. I needed to feel that balance to know if…if what I felt for you was real and not just a rush from the passion and danger." Chloe twisted her fingers in the hem of her T-shirt. Her voice wobbled a bit as she admitted, "I also needed to know if… if you would… well…if you…."

Logan took a step forward and cupped her jaw, tilting her face back. "If I would come after you? Is that what you are trying to say, babygirl?"

Chloe's eyes filled with tears as she nodded. "I began to lose hope," she said forlornly.

Logan took a lock of her hair between his forefinger and thumb and ran them down the silken length, giving it a tug at the end. "Baby, I was on your six before your taxi even got to the car rental place."

Her brow wrinkled as she tried to understand what he was saying. "What do you mean?"

Logan ran his knuckles down her cheek. "How do you

think you were able to get into Canada without a passport?"

"I…I didn't know they'd changed the rules after 9/11 but the border agent took pity on me."

Logan shook his head.

"You?"

"Me. And you think you just found this apartment in one of the safest neighborhoods in Montreal with an easily defended cul-de-sac and a landlord who didn't need a background check?"

"No! I met my landlord in a coffee shop! She said her granddaughter had just gotten married, and she needed a new renter, and she thought I had an honest face."

Logan shook his head again. "Sorry, baby. She's CSIS."

"What the fuck is that?"

"Language," he admonished sternly. "Canadian Secret Intelligence Service."

"My sweet old lady landlord?"

Logan shrugged his shoulders. "It's what makes her so good."

Her lower lip shot out. "What about the jewelry case at the market? I suppose that was you too?"

Logan placed a finger under her chin and forced her to look at him. "That was all you, baby. Hand to God. All you. And I am very proud of you."

She beamed under his praise.

"So you've been here the whole month? Why… why didn't you tell me? Why didn't you—"

"Like you said, you needed to do this. I just couldn't let you do it completely alone. I had to protect my baby."

Chloe's cheeks pinkened. She'd missed him. She'd missed this.

Logan reached down to unbuckle his belt. "Do you know what else I have to do?"

Her stomach flipped as she squeezed her thighs tight. She shook her head as she slid her right foot back one tiny step.

"I have to punish my baby for lying."

"I didn't lie!"

Logan picked up the note she'd written. "'I can't fall in love with you. I can't repeat my past mistakes,'" he read. Holding the note up between two fingers, he raised an eyebrow at her as he accused, "Lie."

"How is that a lie? I was telling you how I felt," she complained.

Logan put down the note and unhooked the top button of his jeans. Chloe took another step back as her eyes widened in anticipation. He then pulled his T-shirt over his head, exposing his cut abs and inked skin.

Chloe licked her lips without thinking.

Logan took another step forward. "It's a lie because we both know you were already in love with me."

Chloe's mouth fell open.

Logan kicked off one boot, then the other. "Say it. You know what I want to hear."

It was time. No more running. No more wondering if she was making a mistake. No more living under the shadow of her past. It was time to face her future. A future with Logan.

"I love you," she responded shyly.

Logan smiled. 'Now we are going to make sure you never forget it."

Chloe bit her lip as he picked up his duffel bag and grabbed her by the upper arm, walking her through the apartment to the bedroom. For half an instant she wondered how he knew his way around but then realized who she was dealing with.

Leading her inside the room, he turned and shut the door. "Strip," he ordered as he walked over to the bed. With one sweep of his arm, he discarded the coverlet, blankets, throw pillows and stuffed animals she had displayed, leaving the bed bare except for the fitted sheet.

With shaking hands, she pulled her T-shirt over her head, self-conscious about her lack of a bra. She raised nervous eyes to him as her arms hovered over her middle, ready to cover herself at the slightest sign of disapproval. His appreciative gaze gave her confidence to reach for the zipper on her jeans. Pulling on the brass tab, the soft, pale skin of her lower abdomen came into view with just a hint of her pink lace panties. Grasping the waistband, she pushed the jeans over the swell of her hips and bottom, letting them slide to the floor.

"The panties too," he ordered gruffly.

Dipping her thumbs into the lace edge, she slowly lowered the flimsy fabric till the faint curls of her pussy were visible. The delicate fabric fell over the bright yellow nail polish covering her toes before she kicked them aside.

"Lie back on the bed and close your eyes."

Chloe hesitantly did as he ordered. The building anticipation for whatever unknown punishment he had planned was twisting her stomach and making it hard for her to breathe. The sheet felt cool against her heated skin as she laid on her back, her arms stiff at her sides.

"Close your eyes and open your legs."

Chloe bit her lip. "Please, please don't…don't use your belt on my pussy," she begged.

The bed dipped as Logan placed a hand on either side of her head and leaned in close. His breath smelled of coffee, his skin the astringent bite of his aftershave. "If I want to take my belt to that pretty little pussy of yours, I will. You have earned this punishment, babygirl, and I won't have you dictating how I deliver it."

"Yes," she whimpered as her fingernails anxiously scraped at the tight-fitting sheet.

"Now open your legs wide."

Chloe reluctantly opened her legs, fighting the urge to place her hands protectively between them. There was a long stretch of silence, then she could hear him moving about the room. The sound of his duffel bag being unzipped. The scrape of a chair. The soft whoosh of his belt being pulled from his jeans belt loops. The hollow metal jangle of the buckle. He must be folding it in half getting ready to punish her, she reasoned as a tear escaped her closed lids. Her apprehension increased with each passing second. It was as if she could feel her heart thudding and thumping in her chest. The blood pumping to every heightened nerve in her body. She dreaded the punishment but craved the absolution through pain it would bring.

Chloe gave out a startled gasp when the cool, silky feel of liquid hit her stomach. "Oh! What?"

"Shhh…" he admonished as the liquid continued to

pour over her stomach, the top of her thighs, her breasts and over her pussy.

The sweet smell of baby powder made her realize he was pouring baby oil on her body.

"Now touch yourself," he commanded.

"Where?" she obediently asked. Her body already responding to the idea of him watching her touch herself as he poured oil over her skin.

"Start with your breasts. Rub the oil in. Test their weight. Pinch your own nipples."

Chloe did as he charged, dipping the edges of her fingertips in the skin-warmed oil. Sliding her fingers through it, she moved her hands in sweeping circles over her flat stomach, edging toward her breasts. Cupping them from the underside, she ran a hand over each breast, coating them in the baby oil, spurred on by the subtle increase in his breathing, a harsh masculine sound in the quiet room. Gently rolling her nipples between her forefingers and thumbs, she felt the nubs harden and become even more sensitive with her touch.

"Move lower. Touch your cunt." His voice raspy and thick as he uttered the dark command.

Instinctively raising her knees, her hands glided down her middle to rest between her thighs. As her fingers began to play over the folds, she could feel warm oil drip down on them.

"That's it, baby. Tilt your bottom up. Display that cunt for me."

Chloe raised her hips, tilting her bottom as she opened her knees wider. Flattening her fingers, she ran her right hand over her pussy, using the top edge of her palm to apply pressure on her clit. She could feel the bed dip. It felt as though he had just knelt between her open legs. Her suspicion was confirmed when she felt his warm hands on her inner thighs. Running them over her, one hand rested on her abdomen, the other over her pussy.

"You look so beautiful. Your creamy skin catches the light and sparkles from the oil as you wait for my next command," he murmured as he pressed the tip of his finger between her folds, circling and teasing her clit.

"Are you going to come for me?"

Chloe nodded her head as she pushed her hips up even higher, grinding against his hand.

"Say it. Say you're going to be a good girl and come for me."

Chloe's voice sounded strained as she panted out, "Please. I will be a good girl. Please! Oh God!"

He pushed two fingers inside her, hooking the tips as he swirled and thrust in a perfect rhythm with the pressure of his thumb against her sensitive nub.

Chloe felt a tightness in her chest. The emotion of feeling his touch almost overwhelming. She'd gone from thinking she might never hear his voice or see his face again to having him here now. Everything from the scrape of his stubble against her cheek, to the rough feel of his hand, to the sound of his voice whispering dark commands...every sensation, every touch, every smell, every sound...affected her. With a cry, she obeyed him. Squeezing her thighs tight, she captured his arm between her legs as she pumped her hips, gripping the sheets. Holding her breath as wave after pleasurable wave washed over her.

"Good girl," he murmured as he caressed her stomach in soothing circles, drawing patterns on her baby-oil-slick skin. "Now, I need you to flip over onto your knees and put your bottom up high in the air. It's time for your punishment."

Chloe's eyes sprang open. "What?"

"You heard me," he said sternly.

"But… but I thought," she stammered.

"You thought what? That because I let you come that you weren't still going to get punished?"

"Well…"

"On your knees."

Chloe flipped onto her stomach then raised up onto her hands and knees.

"Place your cheek on the mattress."

Chloe obeyed. The fragrant scent of baby oil strong as her face brushed the sheets.

She could hear him pop the top on the baby oil, then there was the now-familiar feeling of cool oil dribbling over her skin. It fell over the swell of her bottom and slid down the backs of her thighs.

"Reach back and open your cheeks for me."

A sob escaped her lips as she now guessed his intentions. "Please. I'm not ready."

"You should have thought about that before you didn't trust me and ran away."

With a resigned whimper, she reached back. Placing the tips of her fingers along her curves, she tried to open her bottom cheeks as he instructed, but her skin was too slippery.

"I can't. I can't get a grip."

"You are not trying hard enough. Would you like some help from my belt?"

"No."

Chloe felt a tightening around her shoulder blades as she stretched her arms further, forcing her fingertips deeper between her cheeks, opening them. The moment she was exposed to his gaze, she felt the oil pour over her puckered, hidden hole. It twitched and fluttered as she instinctively clenched that tight, untried entrance. Oh God, she thought. This was happening. He was going to punish her by punishing her asshole.

Chloe pressed her forehead into the mattress as she waited in pained dread. She could hear the rustle of him once again rummaging in his duffel bag.

The bed dipped.

She held her breath.

"Tilt your head to the side and open your eyes."

Chloe moved her head. Logan had removed his jeans. His large shaft was jutting forward. Thick and straight.

"Open your mouth. Nice and wide."

Was he going to make her suck his cock before fucking her ass, she wondered? Reluctantly, she opened her mouth but quickly shut it when she saw what was in his hand. It was a strand of large, purple anal beads. Each of the five balls over an inch and a half in diameter.

Releasing her hold on her buttocks, Chloe used her hands to push herself up. "You can't, Logan! It will hurt too much!" she exclaimed.

His hand fell on her bare bottom with a loud smack.

She could instantly visualize the red handprint that no

doubt bloomed against her ass as the impact of the heated sting spread over her lower back and up her spine.

"I'm sorry I didn't trust you. I'm sorry I ran, but please! Please don't do this. I just can't," she sobbed as her head fell back to the sheets. Her face a mask of despair and fear.

She peeked up at his stern countenance to see if he was moved by her plea. She was met by a cold, hard stare.

"I will give you to the count of two to open your mouth," he cautioned.

Chloe whimpered. Her jaw clenched. She could feel her teeth scrape against one another as she fought against her own unwillingness to accept the punishment he had planned. This was a turning point. She either gave fully of herself and committed to this part of their relationship, or she walked away for good. There was no halfway with a man like Logan. This may have never been her or his kink before, but it was something they now shared. A dynamic they naturally gravitated to. This would be *their* dynamic.

And she wanted it. Wanted all of it. His belt. His punishments. His rules. His commands. She wanted it. Wanted him. Wanted to bend to his will. Wanted to feel his cock push into her as he forcefully took what he wanted from her body. It was through him she could finally let go of her guilt. It was through him and his dominating influence that she could finally move forward with her life. It all came back to him.

By representing the very embodiment of her demons, he had become her avenging angel.

Chloe opened her mouth before he had even said the word "one."

Logan smiled. "Good girl. Now show me how you can suck that ball. Get it nice and wet."

Chloe cringed at the unappealing plastic taste as she accepted the first anal bead into her mouth. Swirling her tongue over the smooth surface, she got it nice and wet for him.

"Now let's see you fit another one in that cute little mouth of yours."

Logan pressed the second purple ball past her lips.

Chloe struggled to move her tongue around the second ball. Her mouth felt awkwardly full.

"And now a third."

Chloe whimpered and tried to protest, but the two large plastic balls in her mouth prevented anything intelligible from escaping. Instead, she tried shaking her head and pleading with her eyes.

He ignored her. He rubbed the smooth surface of the third ball along her lower lip. "Open up."

Chloe opened her lips as wide as she could. One of the balls was sitting in the center of her tongue, preventing him from pushing in the third ball. She secretly hoped he saw that and would give up on the idea of making her suck three balls. She was wrong.

She watched in horror as his arm raised high. Her cries were useless. It was too late. As if in slow-motion, she saw his arm swing in an arc and felt his hand make contact with the vulnerable area above her thigh, but just below the undercurve of her ass. Her sit spot. He didn't stop at one spank but peppered both thighs with a series of brutal slaps. Chloe was sobbing and choking as she tried to scream around the objects in her mouth. Her bottom felt like it was on fire, a thousand hot pin pricks radiating over her skin.

"Is my baby ready to listen?"

Moving her head in an exaggerated motion so he would be left in no doubt of her acquiescence, Chloe nodded an emphatic yes.

"Good. Now push your tongue between the balls and make room for the third one."

She did as she was told, pushing the other two purple balls to the hollows of her cheeks. He placed the third ball in the center of her tongue. Chloe choked but kept the ball tucked in her mouth. It was impossible to move her tongue anymore. She could feel a small dribble of spittle form in the corners of her mouth as she strained to keep the three balls inside. Her cheeks flamed with embarrassment from the image she must have presented with her cheeks pushed out from the anal beads.

Logan ran a hand down her back, caressing her between the shoulder blades before gliding his hand over her bottom. While he'd not admonished her for releasing her hold of her buttocks, that didn't mean he was going to leave them closed. She could feel his fingers press between her cheeks and the tip of his finger circling her puckered hole. He applied subtle force till the oil-slick tip pushed past her feeble resistance and slipped inside. Her body clenched around the intrusive digit.

"Now, I want you to imagine what it is going to feel like when I push each one of the balls up inside your body."

Chloe's eyes grew wide. She made an awkward sucking sound as she struggled to contain the anal beads

RUTHLESS SURRENDER

in her mouth. The image of these large balls inside her tiny bottom made her stomach flip with fear.

"Each ball, one by one, till your bottom feels as full as your mouth does now. Would my babygirl like that?"

Chloe shook her head.

"Does my babygirl deserve it?"

Mournfully, Chloe nodded her head . Yes, she did deserve this punishment and probably more. As much as she feared it, she craved the release only the pain of his punishments could give.

Logan gently pulled on the string, one bead popping free. The second two easily slipped from between her lips.

Chloe buried her face in the sheets as he moved to stand behind her bent form.

She could feel him run the first bead over her lower back. Swirling it in circles over her skin. Coating it with the baby oil already warmed by her own body. With each pass of the bead, the dreadful anticipation increased. Her breath came out in harsh gasps as she waited...waited for her real punishment to begin.

He moved the beads to rest at the top of her ass. After pausing for just a moment, he slid them down the crease. Again, he paused at her pussy entrance. Still sensitive from her recent orgasm, the slight pressure sent a jolt of sensation between her thighs. She felt him move the beads back up the crease. This time applying more pressure so they divided her cheeks. He stopped over her hidden entrance. She could feel him wedge his fingertips between her cheeks and force her left cheek to the side, giving his right hand access to her tight hole. Pressing the top of the first bead against her asshole, he started to push.

Chloe sucked in a breath. Her body resisted. Pushed back. Denied him.

But he would not be rebuffed.

He pushed harder. Her body could not hold back the forced intrusion of the smooth, oiled object. She felt a sharp stab of pain as her entrance opened and the ball was pushed in before her hole quickly closed up around the string. It felt extremely odd. Very different from before, when he'd just pushed the tips of his fingers inside her.

Chloe felt a slight tug on the string before she felt the press of the second ball at her asshole. Gripping the sheets, she tried to accept her punishment but couldn't. Her body still resisted.

"Don't fight me. Do you need another reminder of what happens when you don't give in?"

"No," she whispered. Her voice hoarse from strain.

The second bead pushed against her entrance. Like the first, it slid in the moment her body weakened.

"Oh! Oh! Oh! I... I... it... oh!" Chloe's breath came in sharp gasps as she struggled to put into words how she felt about the unwelcome sensation.

"Remember how full your mouth felt? Remember how you struggled to keep all three balls inside that tiny space?"

"Oh God!" she whined.

Again there was the slight tug of the string before the third ball was pressing for entry. The delicate skin around her back entrance was pinched between the second and third ball. The discomfort causing her body to release and allow the third ball to slip in. She could feel the other two slide deeper into her body. Her hips shifted from side to side as her toes curled. It felt uncomfortable. Full. Wrong.

"Is my babygirl ready to accept the fourth bead?"

"But I thought you were only going to do three," she whined.

"No. I could only fit three in that little mouth of yours without choking you. Your body will accept all five beads."

"No! Please. It already hurts! Five is too many!" she complained.

Chloe could feel the fourth bead being pressed against her body. He was not going to listen to her pleas. She had earned this punishment, and he would see she took it in full measure. The fourth bead pressed. By now the clenching ring of muscle protecting her hidden entrance was weak and ineffective. The fourth bead slid into her body with no resistance. The other beads shifted. Chloe moaned. She could feel her inner muscles cramp as they tightened around the foreign objects. Her stomach twisted. She raised her feet high as her hips fell to the mattress. The tightening of her abdomen the moment her body flattened against the bed only made things worse. She quickly went back up onto her knees, desperate to find some position, some movement that would ease the increasing soreness emanating from deep within her body, but there were none. There was no escape from the intrusion, from the building pain.

"Now the fifth bead."

Chloe started to sob. "No. No! It's full. It's full. It won't fit."

He pressed the final anal bead against her asshole.

Chloe screeched and flattened her hips again. Falling to the bed as she cried with abandon.

"Raise up on your knees," he growled.

"I can't. Please! It's full. You'll tear me."

"Raise up on your knees, or I will rip those beads out of your ass and plow into you with my much thicker, much longer cock. You think you feel full now?" he angrily shouted.

Petrified at the thought of him fucking her bottom with his cock in anger, Chloe quickly obeyed. "Sorry," she sniffled.

Once again, she could feel the bead press against her delicate skin. Then nothing. Her momentary relief was shattered when she felt the bed dip. Turning to look over her shoulder, she saw that he had placed one knee on the bed, between her legs. She could feel him place his free hand on her lower back. Pushing down with his hand, her forced her hips lower which caused her bottom to jut out and up just a little further. The pressure on the bead increased. Chloe gave out a cry of agony as she submitted, and the last bead popped in. Her whole body clenched and twisted. She felt as if her body had been fully taken over.

Possessed.

Dominated.

A humbling mixture of humiliation and pain. No matter how she moved, even when she breathed, she could feel them deep inside her. Solid evidence of his ownership of her and her body.

The bed dipped again. She barely felt it when his hands ran up her thighs and over her bottom. His knees pressed against her own, pushing her legs wider. She then felt the smooth head of his cock at her pussy entrance. She knew it was futile to protest. Reaching up, her hands closed around the iron bars of the headboard. The cold metal gave her strange comfort as she braced for his first thrust.

"Is my babygirl ready for me to fuck her pussy?"

"Oh God, yes."

"Does my babygirl want it to hurt?"

Chloe sucked in a breath. The coarse bluntness of his question catching her off guard but it was the brutal honesty of her answer that shook her to her core.

"Yes, please. Make it hurt!"

His hard cock thrust in.

She thought she had felt full…violated…before, but it did not compare to having both his thick shaft and the five anal beads forced into her tiny body. He pulled out and thrust back in again. She screamed in pain. He thrust again. Then again. And again. The pain twisted, morphed. Her sense of self shattered. She was only her body.

She was only this moment.

There was no past.

Only him.

His fingers dug into her hips as he pounded into her flesh.

"Come for me," he ground out.

She obeyed, never having felt such a soul-stealing, crushing, overpowering orgasm in her life. He had stripped her bare, physically and mentally. And the raw beauty, the raw honesty of it all, allowed her to completely and fully let go. Through the roaring in her ears, she could hear his primal shout before feeling the hot liquid of his come on her back. Her knees gave out. She collapsed on the bed. The heavy weight of his body soon followed. The room was silent except for the intermingled sound of their rapid breaths.

Logan reached down and grabbed a T-shirt that was lying on the floor. He gently wiped it over her back, bottom and thighs. Balling the fabric up and tossing it back on the floor, he turned on his side, bending his elbow and resting his head in his hand to stare at her.

"Well? What did you think of your punishment?"

Chloe gave him a shy smile.

"I think I may be tempted to misbehave again."

This man broke her into tiny pieces only to piece her back together each time he made love to her. It was a scary thing to contemplate. Someone having the power to affect you so deeply they shattered your soul.

"You may want to rethink that." His voice held a hint of amusement.

Catching on to his playful tone, Chloe reached up to run her smooth palm over his rough stubble. "And why is that?"

Logan reached down and gave the anal bead string a sharp tug.

"Because your punishment isn't over. I still have to remove the beads."

Chloe buried her head against his chest. His strong arms wrapped around her, cuddling her close.

His warm hand ran down her back. Once more grasping the string...he pulled. Hard.

***

Hours later, she was tucked on his lap being spoon-fed the chicken noodle soup he had just made for her from scratch. After their mind-blowing sex, he had gently bathed her and placed her in her fuzzy pink footy pajamas. He'd given her a hot cup of tea with extra honey, and she'd sat curled on the sofa, watching him cook the soup in her small kitchen. Then, placing her on his lap, he'd insisted on being the one to feed her.

In the middle of him admonishing her about her horrible eating habits and stating that from this point forward he would see that she ate healthy and took better care of herself, she said, "I really do love you. Well, I mean...I just wanted to say that I didn't just say it earlier for the...just for...you know!"

She waited. Biting her lip anxiously, she wondered how the most powerful and dangerous man she had ever met would feel about a woman dressed in fuzzy pink PJs declaring her love.

He caught a single curl between his finger and thumb and gave it an affectionate tug. "I love you too, babygirl."

Chloe let out the breath she had been holding. Twisting her hands in her lap, she hesitantly asked him a question that had been bothering her. "When we checked into the hotel, how come I saw a 'J' on your credit card?"

Logan smiled. "I knew I couldn't get anything past you. The 'J' stands for Joseph, my first name. I go by my middle name, Logan."

"Oh!"

Chloe was relieved. She knew in time she would ask

him more questions about his past, about what he did for living, but not now. Now, in this moment, the past didn't exist. Only the future, their future, mattered.

Although there was just one more thing she needed to know before they could truly move forward.

After swallowing another savory bite of the warm soup, she said, "May I ask another question?"

"Babygirl, I want no more secrets between us. You may ask me anything you want." His voice was filled with warm, honest affection.

Bolstered by his encouraging tone, she asked, "What is your last name?"

Logan threw his head back with laughter as he hugged her close.

"It's not funny! Do you realize I have no idea who you really are, what your name is?" she complained as she lightly slapped his hard chest.

"You know my name and who I am," he said as he cupped her jaw, staring at her intently with those brilliant blue eyes that always drew her in.

At her questioning look he said, "I'm yours."

EPILOGUE

*L*ogan rolled down the worn cobblestone street. Throwing the kickstand on his Harley Roadster, he took off his helmet and tossed it on the seat. Reaching into his saddlebags, he pulled out a crumpled brown paper bag. Surveying the quiet side street, he took in the cafe to the left of him and the travel bookstore to the right. Ignoring both businesses, he headed straight for the small shop in the center.

His target.

A melodic tinkling chime announced his presence as he walked through the door. The interior was in shadows, emphasizing the pin-point lighting on the various expensive objects displayed in glass cases.

The already hushed atmosphere grew silent at his intimidating approach.

The staff exchanged worried looks.

Disregarding them, he headed straight for the backroom. No one tried to stop him.

Moments before entering he could hear the crumpling

of paper and the slam of a drawer on the other side of the office door. Logan smiled. He always found what he sought. It was pointless to try to hide any secrets from him. Grasping the brass knob, he swung the door open wide.

"Hello, husband! What brings you by?" asked Chloe in a high-pitched tone.

She was sitting primly behind her desk. With him as an investment partner, she had been able to realize her dream of opening a jewelry shop. The Dirty Diamond was a huge success and very popular among the tourists as well as the locals. They were even in the process of expanding the business by creating an online web shop which would feature her own as well as other local artists' jewelry and high-end crafts.

Logan took in her false, innocent look. He always knew when his babygirl was lying. "You forgot the lunch I made you," he said in a light tone, matching her own.

With that, he tossed the brown paper bag onto her desk.

"You're right! I did. How silly of me!" Chloe grimaced as she looked down at the sorry-looking bag sitting on top of her balance sheet. "You really shouldn't have. I know how busy you are."

Logan walked around the desk and sat on the edge, enjoying the anxious look she cast toward the drawer to the left of his thigh.

"Well, I couldn't let my baby go hungry," teased Logan as he tapped the tip of her nose, relishing in her girlish nervousness.

Chloe let out a nervous laugh. "I *was* getting hungry!"

"Really?" asked Logan as he uncrossed his arms. "You sure this cheeseburger and fries weren't filling you up?"

He flicked open the drawer and exposed her dirty secret. A double cheese Black Angus burger with extra pickles and fries slathered with ketchup laid nestled within their greasy paper-wrapping.

Logan trying to get Chloe to eat healthy, and Chloe sneaking junk food despite his strict orders, was a common game they played which often led to some creative punishments. It had been two years since he'd moved to Montreal to be with her and close to one year since they'd married. She continued to entertain and excite him. Life was never boring with Chloe around. Never in his life had he meant anything more than when he'd promised to love and protect her. She was his life. His love. His adorable babygirl.

"Who told on me?" Chloe pouted, then stood up and leaned over her desk to call through the open door, "Marianne, you rat!"

Her friend and shop manager poked her head into the office. Wagging her finger, she said, *"Non! Ne me regarde pas!* You don't have to be married to James Bond to know you have been eating junk food in here! The whole office smells like salt and meat!"

Chloe stuck her tongue out at Marianne, who returned the gesture before laughing and closing the door.

"How many times do you have to tell her I am not a spy?" chuckled Logan.

"It is no use. She won't listen. She loves the romantic idea behind you being an international man of mystery spy, and nothing I say will dissuade her," said Chloe with a shrug of her shoulders.

"Aren't you going to see what I brought you?" Logan gave her a wink as he pointedly removed the burger and fries from her drawer and threw them in the trash.

Chloe cast a forlorn look at her discarded lunch. "It is downright un-American to throw away a perfectly good burger," she grumbled.

"Good thing we are in Canada," he fired back with a laugh.

Casting a stubborn pout his way, she unrolled the top of the paper bag and peeked inside. Lying between a ham and cheese on whole wheat sandwich and a Ziploc bag of carrot and celery sticks was a pair of handcuffs.

Chloe's cheeks blushed as she quickly closed the bag, placing both hands on top for good measure.

"Don't you like your lunch?" Logan pasted on an innocent look as he pried the bag from under her fingers. "Let's see. We have a ham sandwich, and some carrots and celery sticks." He pulled each item out of the bag and placed it before her. Chloe raised wide eyes to him as he pulled the handcuffs out of the bag next and dangled them before her. "And handcuffs. What do these mean, baby?"

"That I was a bad girl," responded Chloe, trying and failing to hide a slight smile.

His bad girl had a habit of trying to cover her bottom when he used his belt on her. To solve the problem, he had taken to handcuffing her whenever she received that particular punishment, something they both enjoyed.

"What do you say?"

"Sorry."

"And what am I going to do about it?" Logan raised an eyebrow as he spread his legs open. The hard outline of his cock was clearly visible as it rested against his inner thigh.

Chloe rose and stepped between his knees. Running her hands up the top of each thigh, she purred into his ear, "You're going to punish me with your big...heavy...belt!" she finished as she brushed her fingertips along his shaft before grasping his belt buckle.

With a growl, Logan notched a shoulder into her stomach and lifted her high. Ignoring her playful shrieks, he strolled out of the office. "Chloe is taking the rest of the day off, Marianne. Hold down the fort."

"Uh huh," responded Marianne, both her and the employee she was instructing barely looking up. They were accustomed to the playful antics of the owners.

Emerging outside, Logan placed Chloe on the back of his motorcycle and handed her her pink helmet.

"Where are we going?" she asked as she buckled the bedazzled strap under her chin.

Logan leaned in to give her lips a hard kiss. "I'm taking you home."

THE END.

ABOUT ZOE BLAKE

Zoe Blake is the USA Today Bestselling Author of the romantic suspense sagas The Diamanti Billionaire Dynasty & The Cavalieri Billionaire Legacy inspired by her own heritage as well as her obsession with jewelry, travel, and the salacious gossip of history's most infamous families.

She delights in writing Dark Romance books filled with overly possessive billionaires, taboo scenes, and unexpected twists. She usually spends her ill-gotten gains on martinis, travels, and red lipstick. Since she can barely boil water, she's lucky enough to be married to a sexy Chef.

ALSO BY ZOE BLAKE

THE SURRENDER SERIES

An Enemies to Lovers Romance

Ruthless Surrender

I know her darkest secret and am just ruthless enough to use it against her.

Whether she likes it or not, I'm the only one who can help her, but I do nothing for free.

My price is her complete surrender.

She can hate me all she wants, as long as she pays with her body.

And if she tries to run?

That will just cost her more.

Rebellious Surrender

First, she tried to kill me.

Then she ran.

Hunting her down will be my pleasure and her pain.

Nobody defies me and gets away with it, especially not her.

My pretty captive is about to learn her rebelliousness has consequences.

I'll settle for nothing less than her complete surrender.

Reckless Surrender

Her first mistake was lying to me.

Did she actually think I would let her get away with this deception?

I was going to make her pay for every lie that slipped from those gorgeous lips.

She may think this is just a game of teacher and naughty schoolgirl, but I have a surprise for her.

I only play games I can win, and my prize will be her complete surrender.

Relentless Surrender

She's mine… she just doesn't know it yet.

Stubborn and feisty as hell, she's going to fight me every step of the way.

What she doesn't understand is, I'm a Marine… and we never back down.

If we see a target we want… we take it.

It's as simple as that.

And I want her.

Badly.

RUTHLESS OBSESSION SERIES

A Dark Mafia Romance

Sweet Cruelty

Dimitri & Emma's story

It was an innocent mistake.

She knocked on the wrong door.

Mine.

If I were a better man, I would've just let her go.

But I'm not.

I'm a cruel bastard.

I ruthlessly claimed her virtue for my own.

It should have been enough.

But it wasn't.

I needed more.

Craved it.

She became my obsession.

Her sweetness and purity taunted my dark soul.

The need to possess her nearly drove me mad.

A Russian arms dealer had no business pursuing a naive librarian student.

She didn't belong in my world.

I would bring her only pain.

But it was too late…

She was mine and I was keeping her.

Sweet Depravity

Vaska & Mary's story

The moment she opened those gorgeous red lips to tell me no, she was mine.

I was a powerful Russian arms dealer and she was an innocent schoolteacher.

If she had a choice, she'd run as far away from me as possible.

Unfortunately for her, I wasn't giving her one.

I wasn't just going to take her; I was going to take over her entire world.

Where she lived.

What she ate.

Where she worked.

All would be under my control.

Call it obsession.

Call it depravity.

I don't give a damn… as long as you call her mine.

Sweet Savagery

Ivan & Dylan's Story

I was a savage bent on claiming her as punishment for her family's mistakes.

As a powerful Russian Arms dealer, no one steals from me and gets away with it.

She was an innocent pawn in a dangerous game.

She had no idea the package her uncle sent her from Russia contained my stolen money.

If I were a good man, I would let her return the money and leave.

If I were a gentleman, I might even let her keep some of it just for frightening her.

As I stared down at the beautiful living doll stretched out before me like a virgin sacrifice,

I thanked God for every sin and misdeed that had blackened my cold heart.

I was not a good man.

I sure as hell wasn't a gentleman… and I had no intention of letting her go.

She was mine now.

And no one takes what's mine.

Sweet Brutality

Maxim & Carinna's story

The more she fights me, the more I want her.

It's that beautiful, sassy mouth of hers.

It makes me want to push her to her knees and dominate her, like the brutal savage I am.

As a Russian Arms dealer, I should not be ruthlessly pursuing an innocent college student like her, but that would not stop me.

A twist of fate may have brought us together, but it is my twisted obsession that will hold her captive as my own treasured possession.

She is mine now.

I dare you to try and take her from me.

Sweet Ferocity

Luka & Katie's Story

I was a mafia mercenary only hired to find her, but now I'm going to keep her.

She is a Russian mafia princess, kidnapped to be used as a pawn in a dangerous territory war.

Saving her was my job. Keeping her safe had become my obsession.

Every move she makes, I am in the shadows, watching.

I was like a feral animal: cruel, violent, and selfishly out for my own needs. Until her.

Now, I will make her mine by any means necessary.

I am her protector, but no one is going to protect her from me.

IVANOV CRIME FAMILY TRILOGY

A Dark Mafia Romance

Savage Vow

Gregor & Samara's story

I took her innocence as payment.

She was far too young and naïve to be betrothed to a monster like me.

I would bring only pain and darkness into her sheltered world.

That's why she ran.

I should've just let her go…

She never asked to marry into a powerful Russian mafia family.

None of this was her choice.

Unfortunately for her, I don't care.

I own her… and after three years of searching… I've found her.

My runaway bride was about to learn disobedience has consequences… punishing ones.

Having her in my arms and under my control had become an obsession.

Nothing was going to keep me from claiming her before the eyes of God and man.

She's finally mine… and I'm never letting her go.

Vicious Oath

Damien & Yelena's story

When I give an order, I expect it to be obeyed.

She's too smart for her own good, and it's going to get her killed.

Against my better judgement, I put her under the protection of my powerful Russian mafia family.

So imagine my anger when the little minx ran.

For three long years I've been on her trail, always one step behind.

Finding and claiming her had become an obsession.

It was getting harder to rein in my driving need to possess her… to own her.

But now the chase is over.

I've found her.

Soon she will be mine.

And I plan to make it official, even if I have to drag her kicking and screaming to the altar.

This time… there will be no escape from me.

Betrayed Honor

Mikhail & Nadia's story

Her innocence was going to get her killed.

That was if I didn't get to her first.

She's the protected little sister of the powerful Ivanov Russian mafia family - the very definition of forbidden.

It's always been my job, as their Head of Security, to watch over her but never to touch.

That ends today.

She disobeyed me and put herself in danger.

It was time to take her in hand.

I'm the only one who can save her and I will fight anyone who tries to stop me, including her brothers.

Honor and loyalty be damned.

She's mine now.

For a list of All of Zoe Blake's Books Visit her Website!

www.zblakebooks.com

Printed in Great Britain
by Amazon